All about the author...
Carol Marinelli

CAROL MARINELLI finds writing a bio rather like
writing her New Year's resolutions. Oh, she'd love to
say that since she wrote the last one, she now goes to
the gym regularly and doesn't stop for coffee, cake and
gossip afterward; that she's incredibly organized and
writes for a few productive hours a day after tidying her
immaculate house and taking a brisk walk with the dog.

The reality is Carol spends an inordinate amount of
time daydreaming about dark, brooding men and
exotic places (research), which doesn't leave too much
time for the gym, housework or anything that comes
in between. And her most productive writing hours
happen to be in the middle of the night, which leaves
her in a constant state of bewildered exhaustion.

Originally from England, Carol now lives in Melbourne,
Australia. She adores going back to the U.K. for a visit—
actually, she adores going anywhere for a visit—and
constantly (expensively) strives to overcome her fear
of flying. She has three gorgeous children who are
growing up so fast (too fast—they've just worked out
that she lies about her age!) and keep her busy with a
never-ending round of homework, sports and friends
coming over.

A nurse and a writer, Carol writes for the Harlequin
Presents and Medical Romance lines, and is passionate
about both. She loves the fast-paced, busy setting of a
modern hospital, but every now and then admits it's
bliss to escape to the glamorous, alluring world of her
heroes and heroines in Harlequin Presents novels. A bit
like her real life, actually!

HARLEQUIN®
Presents

Welcome to the September 2008 collection of
Harlequin Presents!

This month, be sure to read favorite author
Penny Jordan's *Virgin for the Billionaire's Taking*,
in which virginal Keira is whisked off to the exotic
world of handsome Jay! Michelle Reid brings you a
fabulous tale of a ruthless Italian's convenient bride
in *The De Santis Marriage*, while Carol Marinelli's
gorgeous tycoon wants revenge on innocent Caitlyn
in *Italian Boss, Ruthless Revenge*. And don't miss
the final story in Carole Mortimer's brilliant trilogy
THE SICILIANS, *The Sicilian's Innocent Mistress!*
Abby Green brings you the society wedding of
the year in *The Kouros Marriage Revenge*, and in
Chantelle Shaw's *At The Sheikh's Bidding*, Erin's life
is changed forever when she discovers her adopted
son is heir to a desert kingdom!

Also this month, new author Heidi Rice delivers a
sizzling, sexy boss in *The Tycoon's Very Personal
Assistant*, and in Ally Blake's *The Magnate's Indecent
Proposal*, an ordinary girl is faced with a millionaire
who's way out of her league. Enjoy!

We'd love to hear what you think about Harlequin
Presents. E-mail us at Presents@hmb.co.uk or join
in the discussions at www.iheartpresents.com and
www.sensationalromance.blogspot.com, where
you'll also find more information about books and
authors!

Chosen by him for business,
taken by him for pleasure...

A classic collection of office romances from
Harlequin Presents, by your favorite authors.

Look out for more, coming soon!

Carol Marinelli

ITALIAN BOSS, RUTHLESS REVENGE

In Bed WITH THE Boss

HARLEQUIN®

TORONTO • NEW YORK • LONDON
AMSTERDAM • PARIS • SYDNEY • HAMBURG
STOCKHOLM • ATHENS • TOKYO • MILAN • MADRID
PRAGUE • WARSAW • BUDAPEST • AUCKLAND

ISBN-13: 978-0-373-12757-3
ISBN-10:   0-373-12757-X

ITALIAN BOSS, RUTHLESS REVENGE

First North American Publication 2008.

Copyright © 2008 by Carol Marinelli.

www.eHarlequin.com

Printed in U.S.A.

PROLOGUE

'RANALDI'S here!'

A shiver of anticipation went around the lavish hotel reception—starting with a nod from the doorman to warn the concierge, who in turn signalled to the receptionists—and Caitlyn noticed everyone's backs seemed to straighten just a touch more, hands all moving to flatten ties or hair, as a sleek limousine pulled up outside.

'The question is—' Glynn, the manager, blinked nervously as he flicked his fringe back off his face '—which one?'

The answer was, for Caitlyn, more relevant than Glen could possibly realise.

Here on work experience, shadowing the staff and completely supernumerary, it shouldn't have mattered a jot to Caitlyn *which* one of the dashing Ranaldi twins was pulling up outside—after all, both were legends.

Lazzaro and Luca Ranaldi both headed up the sumptuous Ranaldi chain of luxurious international hotels—and, along with their sister, were heirs to the vast wealth their father had created and subsequently, following his death last year, left behind.

Impressive? Yes.

Newsworthy? No.

Unless, of course, that vast wealth happened to have landed in the laps of stunning identical twins. Not one but two immaculate prototypes, who regularly hit the headlines courtesy of their jet-setting, depraved existence. Since their father's death, and their sister marrying and settling there, the stunning pair had loosely based themselves in Melbourne— two irrepressible playboys, who made no apologies and certainly offered no excuses! Only last week Luca had been in the papers for a fight at the casino, and there had been a few drink-driving scandals recently that Caitlyn could recall.

A dark-suited man stepped out of the limousine, and Caitlyn found herself holding her breath…

'Which one is it?' Caitlyn whispered.

'I'm not sure yet…' Glynn mused. 'They're both identical, both divine…'

Caitlyn hoped it was Lazzaro.

Not because he was considered the most powerful, the true leader of the two, but for a reason Glynn would have trouble believing.

Watching as two strappy sandals hit the ground beneath the car door, Caitlyn chewed on her lip, wondering what on earth she'd do if Roxanne came into view—wondering how the other hotel staff would react to her if they knew the strange truth…

Luca Ranaldi was dating her cousin.

'It's Lazzaro,' Glynn confirmed as, without waiting for his date, the dark-suited male walked through the gold revolving doors.

'How do you know?' Caitlyn frowned. 'I thought you said they were identical…'

'Lazzaro doesn't wait for anyone...' Glynn hissed out of the side of his mouth before stepping forward to greet his boss. 'Not even a beautiful woman!'

Oh, she'd seen him before—had seen him in the papers, his photo being on the cover of a business magazine she was reading for her course—but nothing, *nothing* had prepared Caitlyn for the impact of seeing him up close and in the flesh. Well over six feet, as he walked in it was clear to all that he owned the place—and not just literally. Confidence and arrogance just oozed from him, and as he walked over to the desk Caitlyn realised he wasn't just stunning—he was absolutely beautiful. His jet hair was longer than it was in the photos, with a raven fringe flopping over his forehead, and as for those eyes... Caitlyn actually gave a little sigh. Thickly lashed, they were black as the night and just as dangerous. As his gaze met hers, it was bored, utterly uninterested and he soon looked away. But, for Caitlyn, it was as if his image had been branded on her brain, freeze-framed so she could examine it at her leisure—see again that straight Roman nose, see close up his smooth olive skin and that sulky, full, incredibly kissable mouth.

Realising she was staring—gaping, even—Caitlyn tore her gaze away and looked at the woman who had walked in behind him. She was now sitting on one of the plush lobby sofas as she awaited her master—and Caitlyn couldn't help the tiny ironic smile that pursed her lips.

Though it wasn't Roxanne, it might just as well have been.

The raven beauty who accompanied Lazzaro certainly hadn't been striving to achieve *au naturelle* when she'd applied her make-up. Dark glossy hair tumbled, albeit strategically, over shoulders that were so evenly tanned it could only have come from some serious hours on a sunbed combined with a regular spray tan.

'Welcome, sir.' Glynn's outstretched hand went ignored.

'How are things?' Lazzaro didn't return the greeting, his eyes narrowing as they scanned the reception area. 'Any problems?'

'None at all,' his manager assured him.

'Has Luca been in?'

'Not as yet,' Glynn said, discreetly omitting to mention the drunken call he'd taken earlier, demanding that the best room in the hotel be somehow vacated and prepared for his arrival.

'How's the wedding?'

'Excellent,' Glynn enthused. But as Lazzaro's burning gaze fell on him, he coloured up just a touch. 'Well, there's one teeny problem, but we're taking care of it now.'

Lazzaro raised one perfectly arched black brow, and, though he didn't say a word, the tiny gesture clearly indicated that he wanted more information.

'The bride's father, Mr Danton—'

'Gus Danton is a close personal friend of mine,' Lazzaro interrupted, and though his English was excellent, his deep, heavily accented voice held just a tinge of warning.

Caitlyn's eyebrows shot up just a fraction—after all, if he was such a good friend, how come Lazzaro hadn't been at the wedding? She didn't say it, of course, but Lazzaro was either a skilled mind-reader or had felt the breeze from her eyebrows raising, because, as if answering her very thoughts he deigned to give her a brief look.

'There are not enough Saturday nights in a year to attend

every wedding to which I am invited but—given Mr Danton has chosen my hotel, and given Mr Danton is a friend—naturally I will come in for a drink. Of course, I hoped to hear there have been no problems...'

'Quite.' Glynn swallowed.

'So?'

'Well, he's asked that the bar remain open for another hour. Of course we're more than happy to oblige—it's just that his credit card has been declined. I was actually on my way to have a discreet word with him now.'

'Bring up his details.' He snapped his fingers in Caitlyn's vague direction, and even though she'd been bringing up guests' details for most of the night, this *almost* mastered skill had never been tested under such stressful conditions.

'Er, Caitlyn's only here on work experience, sir,' Glynn said, rushing over to the computer. One black look from Lazzaro halted him. 'She's studying hospitality, and—'

'Since when has a work experience student stayed till midnight on a Saturday?' Lazzaro cut in, staring at her name badge, lowering his eyes to her suede stilettos, and then lazily working them upwards—taking in the rather cheap navy skirt and white blouse that comprised her uniform. In absolutely no hurry, as Glynn chatted nervously on, he scrutinised her face, staring into her blue eyes and doing the strangest things to her stomach.

'Caitlyn was very keen to witness a busy Saturday night...'

God, she wished she'd had warning—wished she'd had time to dash to the loo and redo her heavy blonde hair. She could feel her attempt at a French roll uncoiling before his eyes. And she wished the mouth he was staring at had just a little bit of lipstick on.

'And she has been dealing with guests?'

'Yes,' Glynn croaked. 'Well, she's been closely supervised, of course.'

'She has been bringing up details for paying guests?'

'Er, yes…' Glynn nodded. 'But, as I said, only with supervision.' Which wasn't strictly true—Glynn had been out for more smoke breaks than Caitlyn could count. Still, she was hardly going to tell Lazzaro that.

'If she is good enough for my guests,' Lazzaro responded, with the martyrdom only the truly pompous could muster, 'then she is good enough for me.'

If he called her *she* again, Caitlyn decided, then *she'd* jolly well give him a piece of her mind.

As his black eyes fell on her, Caitlyn recanted.

Well, maybe she wouldn't actually *say* anything. Still, she could *think* it—divine he might be to look at, but he was a loathsome, arrogant, chauvinist brute. Blushing with a mixture of annoyance and embarrassment, she furiously backspaced as she spectacularly mistyped. After an exceedingly long moment, Gus Danton's details finally flashed on to the screen.

Momentarily!

'His account,' Lazzaro snapped, clearly expecting that with a few rapid clicks Caitlyn should bring up the necessary page. But his impatience only unsettled her more.

The cursor wobbled on screen as suddenly he was behind her, standing over her, his hand hovering to take the computer mouse—effectively dismissing her efforts. She should have stepped back—only he was behind her. She should have moved her hand to let him take over—only his was above hers.

Perhaps it was the prospect of physical contact with him, perhaps it was nerves, or an impossible combination of both, but at *that* second precisely her hope for a glowing reference from the Ranaldi Hotel for her work experience melted away as rapidly as Caitlyn clicked the mouse—not once, not twice, but as if her finger had suddenly developed a nervous twitch. She repeatedly tapped away—panic rising as she deleted Lazzaro Ranaldi's number-one guest's entire financial history before his very eyes. He should step in, Caitlyn thought, frantically hitting the back arrow, sweat trickling between her breasts as his hand still hovered. His breath was on the back of her burning neck as an unfamiliar system command popped on screen, to taunt her.

Put Susan to Bed.

What?

Oh—she should have pressed cancel. As soon as she tapped okay, Caitlyn recalled the meaning of the strange prompt—that she really *didn't* want the computer system to shut down on the day, that she really, *really* didn't want to do the *one single thing* Glynn had told her she must never, ever do. But as the screen went black, Caitlyn knew that Susan wasn't just in bed, she was snoring her head off and completely unrousable as somewhere in the system she tallied and recorded the day's figures and guests' comings and goings.

Caitlyn never swore—well, never in front of her boss— but her curse was out before she could stop it. Glynn's alarmed expression told her that her frantic whisper had reached his ears.

'Everything okay?' Glynn checked nervously, from the other side of the desk, and Caitlyn looked up to face the lesser of two evils but Glynn's visible terror at her horrified expression held nothing that could console her. 'Everything is okay, isn't it?' he hissed.

'There seems to be a problem with the system.' Caitlyn attempted a calm voice, only her mouth seemed to belong to someone who had just stepped out of the dentist's after having a root canal procedure. Her lips struggled to form the words, her finger was still tapping away, but her whole body was absolutely rigid. She was wishing that she'd gone home when she could have—when she *should* have.

'What the hell do you mean?' Glynn snapped, moving to race his way around the counter. 'A problem with the system? What on earth have you done, Caitlyn?'

Ended her career before it had even started, probably, Caitlyn thought with dread. Lazzaro Ranaldi's temper was legendary amongst the staff—and something she'd never wanted to witness, particularly aimed at herself. Bracing herself for his caustic tongue, for a few choice expletives to fill the lavish reception area as he told her exactly what he thought of her computer skills, of her woeful inadequacy to work for such an exclusive hotel, bravely— *stupidly*, perhaps—Caitlyn lifted her head and craned her neck to face him.

Her terrified expression turned to one of bemusement as she saw that the eyes that met hers weren't hostile at all. In fact, if she wasn't mistaken, there was just the hint of a smile playing on the edge of his mouth.

'It's fine, Glynn.' With one perfectly manicured hand he halted his manager's progress. 'You have guests to attend to.' Lazzaro's eyes fell on a rather affectionate couple at the desk, who really should get a room as quickly as possible. 'As Caitlyn said, there is a small problem with the system—nothing I can't sort.'

Was there really a problem with the system? Caitlyn wondered hopefully as Glynn went to sort out the couple, her eyes darting back to the now flickering screen of the computer.

'Nothing that can't be fixed…' He was leaning right over her now, as she stood frozen to the spot—and not just her feet. Caitlyn's hand was still clutching the mouse like a frozen claw. Her throat tightened as his warm hand closed around hers, guiding it up to the little red arrow at the top and closing the programme—something Caitlyn was sure, positive in fact, that you shouldn't do. Her heart was thumping in her chest as he removed his hand—she should really step aside. Only she didn't. In fact, still she stood there, as his hands came around either side of her waist and moved to the keyboard. Her heart leapt up into her mouth as, without a single mistake, he calmly logged in and with impressive speed typed in the necessary details to retrieve Gus Dalton's information.

'Luckily everything is backed up.' His voice was low in her ear, and she waited for relief to flood her—waited for grateful breath to escape her lips as the crisis was averted. Only it never came. Her body was resisting the call to relax, and her mind was telling her in no uncertain terms that now certainly wasn't the time for complacency. Every nerve was on high alert, every cell, every shred of DNA was quivering with tension. Only it had nothing to do with her career, nothing to do with her boss catching her making a stupendous mistake, but everything to do with the man who was leaning over her, the heavy scent of him, the absolute undeniable maleness of him, was having the most dizzying effect.

'How…?' Caitlyn blinked. 'Glynn said that once Susan was put to bed…'

'All the day's data is sent to me for checking,' Lazzaro explained then elaborated, still tapping away. 'Nothing that happens on this computer is deleted till I am satisfied it is okay…'

'Thank goodness for that.'

'So long as you're not attempting a dash of embezzlement…?' He'd stopped typing now, put the delicious prison of his arms down as he stepped back, and Caitlyn thankfully exhaled before she turned to face him.

'Of course not!' Caitlyn giggled.

'Or having a few friends paying mate's rates while staying in the Presidential Suite?'

'Please!' Caitlyn laughed.

'Or mooning behind the desk checking e-mails and doing a spot of internet banking on my time?'

'Er, no.' Caitlyn wasn't laughing now. In fact she was having trouble forcing a smile.

'Or checking your horoscope…?'

Caitlyn didn't even attempt a denial. Her face was burning an unattractive shade of scarlet, but if she'd had the nerve to look up she'd have seen that he was smiling.

'Everything in order?' Glynn was positively dripping with nerves as he came over.

'Of course.' Lazzaro shrugged. 'I see that Gus paid in advance forty-eight hours before the reception…'

'Still…' Glynn cleared his throat. 'I thought I ought to warn him…'

'Lazzaro!' Smiling, loud, and as red in the face as Caitlyn, Gus Danton crossed the foyer. 'Come in and have a drink!'

'I was just about to.' Lazzaro nodded. 'I trust everything has gone smoothly tonight?'

'It's been perfect!' Gus enthused. 'Everything's gone off without a hitch. Actually…' Gus turned to address Glynn. 'Did you sort out the bar, like I asked?'

'All done,' Lazzaro answered for his manager. 'You'll be posted an itemised bill next week.'

'Details, details…' Gus waved them away. 'Join us, Lazzaro.'

'I'll be there in just a moment.'

As Gus headed back to the ballroom, Lazzaro gave a nod to his waiting beauty. And though he didn't whistle, though he didn't wave a lead, as she jumped up eagerly, the only thing Caitlyn could liken her to was an over-eager dog, finding out it was about to be walked.

Every staff member stood rigid, every polished smile was perfectly in place as he stalked towards the ballroom, yet, like a leaky balloon, one could almost feel the tension seeping out as the ballroom doors were opened and Lazzaro and his date entered. But just as shoulders drooped, just as everyone prepared to exhale *en masse,* as if having second thoughts, he turned around—striding back to the reception desk and fixing a stunned Caitlyn with his stern glare.

'Why did I do that?' he demanded. 'Come on—you are here to learn. Why, when this is a business, when I know he may not have the funds, would I choose, for now, to ignore it?'

'Er…' Caitlyn's eyes darted to Glynn's in a brief plea for help, but when none was forthcoming she forced herself to look back at Lazzaro. 'Because he's a friend?' Caitlyn attempted. Seeing his frown deepen, she had another stab. 'Because he's a guest and, rather than embarrass him tonight…' The frown was still deepening as she frantically racked her brain. 'Because he's already paid so much…'

She was clearly completely off track. Her mind raced to come up with an answer, only she had none left. Bracing herself for the cracking whip of his putdown, she gave in. And he did the strangest, most unexpected thing.

'All good reasons. But…' That inscrutable, scathing expression slipped like a mask and broke into another smile of which Caitlyn was the sole beneficiary, and it was like stepping out into the sun unprotected— dazzling, warming, blinding her with its intensity, knocking her completely off guard, a smile that magnified everything. 'He has three more daughters and all of them are single—so if tonight goes well, that is three more weddings…'

He didn't finish. Bored now, he turned again and headed back to his date, and towards the ballroom.

And this time, for Caitlyn at least, the tension had only just started—and there wasn't a trace of breath left in her lungs to be let out.

There were several clocks in the reception area, each giving the different times around the world—ten minutes to midnight in Melbourne, ten minutes to two in the afternoon in London, and ten minutes to nine in the morning in New York—and Caitlyn glanced up at them, freeze-framing them in her mind. Because suddenly it was relevant; for the first time in her life Caitlyn actually understood the saying that time stood still…

Because it did.

At ten minutes to midnight Caitlyn's eyes were dragged back to Lazzaro's departing back, watching as he walked into the ballroom and out of her view, taking with him just a little piece of her very young, very tender heart.

'You might as well go home,' Glynn said a little while later. 'There's not much to do.'

'There will be, though.' Caitlyn coloured up a touch, her work ethic for once having nothing to do with her wanting to hang around. 'Once the wedding reception finishes.'

'It's all under control.'

'What are you going to do about Luca?' Caitlyn asked. 'All the best rooms are booked out for the wedding.'

'He'll be so wasted he won't notice if I put him in the broom cupboard.' Glynn rolled his eyes, then smiled. 'Have you thought about what I said? About working here while you study? A lot of our chambermaids are students.'

Caitlyn nodded. 'I'm going to put in my résumé on Monday.'

'Well, you can put me down as a reference,' Glynn said. 'You've done really well—here.' He handed her a cab voucher.

'What's this for? You don't have to do that!'

'Don't worry—I haven't gone soft. Lazzaro insists the hotel pays for a taxi if staff work after eleven—and given that you're practically staff, he wouldn't hear otherwise!'

'So he can be nice, then?' Caitlyn fished. 'Despite what everyone says?'

'Unfortunately, yes.' Glynn sighed. 'Which means one always ends up forgiving him when he's being bloody! Night, Caitlyn.'

Chatting idly to the doorman, Caitlyn shivered—not with cold but with tiredness as she waited for ever for her taxi. But her weariness was quickly forgotten when Lazzaro's rather ravishing date came out alone and boot-faced, and was gobbled up by his limousine.

'Lovers' tiff.' Geoff winked, once she was safely off into the night. 'You'd think he'd have had the sense to wait till morning to get rid of her!'

'Have they been together long?' Caitlyn attempted to be casual but her face was burning.

'Never seen her till tonight,' Geoff said cheerfully. 'I'll give your taxi another reminder—mind you, the tennis is on. Why don't you wait inside and I'll call you when it comes?'

And she would have—only Lazzaro Ranaldi himself was coming through the revolving glass doors. Lazzaro Ranaldi himself was smiling at her as he walked past.

'You're either very late leaving, or arriving incredibly early.'

'I'm waiting for a taxi,' Caitlyn mumbled.

'You'll be waiting a while—the night match at the tennis just wrapped up.'

'I heard.'

'Would you like a lift?'

Just like that he said it—just like any *normal* person would say it. Only he wasn't just a normal person, and Caitlyn had difficulty coming up with a normal answer. She just stood there mute for a moment as a few hundred thousand dollars' worth of sleek silver sports car pulled up and the valet handed him the keys.

'I was expecting the limousine!' She put on a plummy voice and raised her nose in distaste at his stunning car—then panicked that he wouldn't get her rather offbeat humour.

'Sorry about that… You'll just have to slum it in this…' He didn't just get it, he topped it! As Geoff opened the passenger door for her, Lazzaro peered inside at the immaculate leather upholstery. 'I can look in the boot for a newspaper or something for you to sit on, so you don't mess up your skirt.'

'I'll be fine.' Caitlyn gave a martyred sigh and climbed into the seat, wriggling down in the baby-bottom-soft leather and returning his smile as he joined her, watching as he punched her address into the sat nav. And just like that she forgot to be nervous—just like that they purred off into the night, chatting about anything and everything—including her age.

'How old are you, then?' Lazzaro asked as she rattled on about her studies.

'Twenty,' Caitlyn lied. Then, realising he could look it up, she recanted. 'Well, I will be on Thursday.'

He made a mental note to tell his PA to send flowers and book a table—Thursday suddenly seemed an impossibly long way off.

Turn left at the next roundabout and your destination is on the right,' came the very calm voice of the sat nav.

'The trouble with these things,' Lazzaro said, smiling as he turned off the engine and faced her, 'is that you can't pretend you're lost and prolong your journey.'

'I know where I live,' Caitlyn pointed out, but her heart was soaring at his blatant flirt.

'Nice place.' It was—a massive old weatherboard in a very nice street, just a stone's throw from the beach. Either there were a thousand students crammed in or, Lazzaro realised, she still lived at home. 'Someone's still up.'

'My mum!' Caitlyn frowned at the twitching curtain, wishing she'd just gone to bed, embarrassed all of a sudden and feeling about twelve years old. 'Or my grandad.'

Only it didn't bother him a bit—in fact, there was a certain novelty to it all. Lazzaro was used—too used—to sophisticates seductively inviting him up, having already gone down!

'Then you'd better go in.'

He watched her face fall an inch, and, though he wanted nothing more than to reach over and kiss her, Lazzaro knew exactly how to keep a woman wanting more.

God, she was gorgeous, though, Lazzaro thought as she walked up her drive.

The front door was opening before she even got there.

Funny too, Lazzaro mused, smiling as he drove off into the night. He'd put her out of her misery and ring her on Monday—put himself out of his misery too, Lazzaro thought, shifting uncomfortably in his seat.

Once he'd dealt with Luca he'd ring her.

Luca.

His face hardened when he thought of his twin brother—he was not relishing a bit the task that lay ahead.

Monday suddenly seemed impossibly close.

CHAPTER ONE

'YOU bit him!' Black eyes fixed her with a stern glare as she stood at his desk. *This* was the very last thing Lazzaro needed to be dealing with today, and a petty row among the domestic staff was something he didn't usually have to.

'I didn't bite him,' Caitlyn snapped, and Lazzaro actually blinked. Her denial was not what he had been expecting—especially given the evidence. But her irritation, her indignation, even, told him that this five-minute problem that had landed on his desk at five p.m. on a hellish Friday was actually a rather more serious one. Jenna, his PA, had tearfully resigned on Wednesday, and *her* assistant was off with the flu that had swept through half his admin staff, which meant that today Lazzaro was dealing with what was usually expertly delegated. Only maybe it was just as well he was dealing with this particular scenario. It would seem that Caitlyn—he glanced down at the file on his desk—Caitlyn Bell, had a side to her story that he needed to hear.

Even if he really didn't want to.

'It was just a little nip.' China-blue eyes held his—eyes

that were familiar somehow…eyes that were just as blue as Roxanne's.

Where the hell had *that* thought come from?

This woman was nothing like Roxanne.

Caitlyn was as blonde as Roxanne was dark, and the woman who stood before him was petite whereas Roxanne was curvaceous, but those eyes… A tiny swallow was the only evidence of his inner turmoil—he was angry with himself that even after all this time the memories, the pain, could still wash over him at the most unexpected of times.

'It's not as if I sank my teeth in.'

Lazzaro dragged his mind back to the conversation, grateful to escape his own thoughts, and it was quite hard not to smile at her description, quite hard *not* to compare it to Malvolio's—who had roared and ranted so loudly, his hand wrapped in a handkerchief, as if it was about to fall off. He hadn't known what to expect when he'd called her to his office. He was the last person who would normally deal with one of the hotel's maids, and when he did they were usually cowering in the chair. But not this one.

She'd declined his offer to sit, and was instead standing at his desk—jangling with nerves, perhaps, but curiously strong. Long blonde hair that was presumably usually neatly tied back was tumbling out of its hair-tie after the *incident,* her arms were folded across her chest, and the blue eyes were glassy from her trying not to cry. She kept sniffing in the effort not to, and somehow, even if she was tiny, even if she was clearly shaken, somehow she was incredibly together too—her rosebud mouth pursed and defiant as she refused to relent.

'I need more information.'

'I really don't see what all the fuss is about.'

'One of my staff members has been bitten by another—'

'Not just any one of your staff members…'

This time he deliberately didn't blink. He held his expression in absolute check as she interrupted, and, though few usually dared, he let the fact go as Caitlyn Bell got straight to the rather awkward point.

'Malvolio is, I believe, your brother-in-law.'

He gave a terse nod—a nod that was actually respectful, acknowledging what she had to say even while quickly disregarding it. 'The fact Malvolio is my brother-in-law has no bearing in this matter—none whatsoever. Now, I want to hear exactly what happened.'

'As Malvolio said, we were discussing a promotion—he tripped and, like a reflex action, he put out his hands to save himself—'

'Caitlyn—' Rather more usually, it was Lazzaro interrupting now, but unusually someone overrode him—someone's voice got a touch louder and more insistent as Caitlyn spoke over him.

'And—like a reflex action—I bit him.' She gave a tight smile. 'Or rather, I gave him a little nip.'

'I want the truth.'

'You just got it.'

'Caitlyn, you are one of my staff…'

'Not any more.' She shook her head. 'I just resigned.'

'No.' He wasn't having it—he saw just a flash of tears in those stunning blue eyes, and loathed Malvolio for causing them. 'You do not have to lose your job over this…'

'I was already leaving. That's why I was having a discussion with Malvolio in the first place. I've got an inter-

view next week—a second interview, actually—for a PR
position with the Mancini chain of hotels.'

'A PR position?' Lazzaro frowned. Alberto Mancini
was both his friend and his rival. Both had hotels all over
the world, both had formidable reputations, and both were
choosy with their staff—and a chambermaid, no matter
how well presented, wouldn't cut it in PR. 'You are a chambermaid. How can you have an interview for a PR—?'

'I've been working as a maid while studying.'

'Studying?'

'Hospitality and tourism…'

He was only half listening—that jolt of recognition he
had experienced when he saw her was explained now. That
was where he knew her from. She'd been on the desk—
funny that he could remember, but he did—and there had
been a wedding… The Danton wedding…that was it…

'You did work experience here while you were
studying?' Lazzaro checked. 'A couple of years ago?'

'That's right…' Caitlyn blinked, stunned that he remembered, wondering *what* he remembered. 'Just for a
few days. I filled in an application form at the time, and
I've been working as a maid while I've been studying
ever since.'

He ran a hand over his forehead and trailed it down over
his cheek, fingering for just a second the livid scar that ran
the length of it. And for the second time in as many moments,
Lazzaro came up with another logical explanation as to why
this particular woman's face remained in his memory.

Before.

The weekend before it had happened.

The weekend before, when life had been so much easier.

When laughing had come so much more readily.

He'd kissed thousands of women he couldn't recall. Funny that he remembered one that he hadn't.

'Why haven't you applied for a position here—given your history with the place?'

It was a perfectly reasonable question, one that her family and colleagues regularly asked, but one she simply couldn't answer—and especially not to Lazzaro.

How could she tell him that for more than two years he'd been on her mind, that the king-size crush that had hit her that night—despite her busy life, despite dancing and fun and boyfriends—still hadn't faded?

That she really needed to get a life.

One away from Lazzaro Ranaldi and the stupid torch she carried for him.

Maybe if his brother hadn't died…maybe if she hadn't started work as a chambermaid…maybe if he hadn't been linked with Roxanne and it hadn't been on every news bulletin and in every paper or magazine Caitlyn had opened…then, after that initial meeting, she'd have moved quickly on, forgotten the feel of his eyes on hers, forgotten the thrill in her stomach as that dark, ruthless face had been softened by a rare smile. Only in the days after that meeting she'd seen the pain in those closed features screaming from the newspapers, had winced at the scurrilous gossip that had ensued, the blistering row between brothers that had preceded Luca Ranaldi's sudden and tragic death. But still working in the hotel—instead of moving on—she had caught her breath whenever she'd gleaned an occasional glimpse of him striding through the hotel, blushing in her maid's uniform as—naturally—he didn't deign to give her a glance. Though Caitlyn did. That perfect face, marred since that tragic day by a livid scar along his cheek, with lines now fanning his dark eyes and his mouth permanently set on grim. She could see the tension he carried in his shoulders, and wanted somehow for him to smile again.

Just the way he once had.

She hadn't spoken to him since that night—not even once. And thank goodness for that, Caitlyn realised, because despite more than two years between drinks, so to speak, still he absolutely moved her. Despite the angry scar on his cheek, despite the closed, much more guarded expression he wore now, despite the pain in his eyes—still he was absolutely beautiful.

'I need a bit more variety…' Caitlyn answered truthfully—because she did. She needed to sample a world that didn't have his name on every sheet of paper, needed to check her bank balance and not see 'Ranaldi', needed to just get over him—for good.

'You'll find nowhere better than right here.'

'You're probably right…' Caitlyn's face twisted slightly at the unwitting irony of his statement. 'But I really think it's time for a change—so you see today really doesn't matter. I was leaving soon anyway.'

'But it *does* matter, Caitlyn. You have worked for this hotel for two years and one month.' He gave a small swallow as her eyes narrowed, and he glanced again at her file, as if he'd gleaned the information from there. Only he hadn't—the date was indelibly etched on his mind, but she didn't need to know why…

It had nothing to do with her.

'If anything untoward has happened, you have the same

rights as any other staff member. Just because Malvolio is family…'

'I hear your sister's having a baby…' She pulled a crumpled tissue out of her pocket and gave her nose a rather loud blow.

'What does that have to do with this?' Lazzaro's voice was completely even, his face impassive, but he had to stop himself from drumming his fingers on the desk—actually had to remind himself to keep looking her in the eye as she voiced his very thoughts. How the hell would Antonia cope? She had just started to get her life back on track after Luca's death, the new baby was due in just a few days, there was his niece, Marianna, just four years old—what the hell had Malvolio been *thinking?*

'It has everything to do with this!' Caitlyn gulped. 'Look, I'm fine—I really am—and I don't want any fuss. I just want to get my things and leave.'

And, though it must surely be the last thing she wanted after the day's events, all *he* wanted to do was to walk around the desk and put his arms around her, this little spitfire who had marched into his office on his command and was about to walk out against it. And, yes, technically it would be so much easier to let her go. But it would be wrong, so very wrong, if he did.

'Caitlyn—let's just talk about this. It can be dealt with—you really do not have to leave.'

'Oh, but I think I do,' she countered. 'As I said, I've got the Mancini interview…I can muddle through till then. Though…' Her voice faded, her head shaking at the impossibility of explaining her problems to him.

'What?'

'It's complicated.'

'Probably not to me.'

She managed a wan smile, realising she had no choice but to tell him. 'I've been doing a lot of overtime for the last two months. A *lot* of overtime,' Caitlyn reiterated.

'I will ensure that you're paid.'

'It's just that…' Caitlyn took a deep breath. 'I'm applying for a mortgage, and I need three months of payslips to show my earnings.' She scuffed the carpet with her foot. 'I told the bank it was my regular wage.'

'Without overtime?' Lazzaro checked. 'But wouldn't that show up on your payslip?'

'Quite!' Caitlyn blushed.

'So you lied to the bank?'

'Not lied exactly.' Caitlyn gulped. 'Malvolio said it…' She watched his eyes narrow, realised he must be thinking there was something more to their working relationship. There truly wasn't. She had asked and he had agreed—it was as simple as that. 'Oh, it doesn't matter.' Caitlyn shrugged. 'I need three payslips anyway.'

'Then stay.'

'I don't want to.' She stood firm. 'I'd rather not put Malvolio down as a reference. I know he deals with the domestic staff, and I know he usually would be the one, but I…'

'You can put me—I can assure you I have more influence with Mancini than Malvolio does, and I will ensure it is extremely favourable.'

'How?' Caitlyn frowned. 'How can you write my reference when you don't know anything about me?'

'Oh, but I think I do.' Her words, only spoken through

his lips now. He stared over at her—little, but strong and, unlike his brother-in-law, unlike the father of the baby, this stranger actually gave a damn about the woman who was carrying his child.

'I will get the forms and have your pay made up. I will do it on Monday—that way, if you change your mind over the weekend—'

'Could you get the forms now, please?' She wasn't looking at him now, instead staring out of his vast windows somewhere over his shoulder at the Melbourne city skyline. 'I won't be changing my mind.'

'Just think about it.'

'I'd like the forms now.'

This time she didn't add please.

This time Lazzaro knew there was no persuading her otherwise.

'Where's Malvolio?'

Storming through the Admin corridors, Lazzaro caught everyone by surprise. Admin staff with bags over their shoulders, hoping to slope off a little early, suddenly sat back down and started tapping at blank screens; the raucous laughter coming from the boardroom that signalled end-of-week drinks that Lazzaro supplied for his team, which should start at five but in fact seemed to start around lunchtime, snapped off as if the power had been pulled as he stormed into rather unfamiliar territory. His suite was on the top floor, and he had a private lift that absolutely bypassed the usually well-oiled engines of Admin.

But come five p.m. on Friday, the wheels fell off somewhat!

'He's gone!' Audrey Miller, Malvolio's assistant, gave an anxious smile. 'He had to dash off—Antonia rang and said she was having some cramps…'

'Antonia's in labour?'

'I'm not sure.' Audrey gulped. 'But the staff got a bit excited, as you can see…'

There wasn't a hope in hell of getting the termination forms—let alone a final cheque cut.

He'd deal with the lot of them on Monday.

Right now, his sister could be in labour.

His brother-in-law by her side.

The same brother-in-law who had forced Caitlyn Bell's resignation for all the wrong reasons.

CHAPTER TWO

Damn!

Pacing the floor of the huge office, Caitlyn paused for a moment to blow her nose again, and rummaged in her bag for her compact, powdering her reddened face and telling herself to hold it together for just a little while longer.

She'd surely get another job—but she also needed those three blasted payslips just in case the court ruling went against her mother.

It wouldn't, Caitlyn consoled herself. Their lawyer had assured them that everything was under control. A moan of horror escaped her lips at the thought of that same lawyer's bill, sitting on the dining room table—a bill that had to be paid before he'd proceed further.

What the hell was she going to do?

She'd lied to Lazzaro about a second interview with the Mancini chain—she hadn't even had the first interview yet. Her application was still sitting half-typed on her computer! Actually, she'd lied to Lazzaro about everything. There had been no discussion about a promotion; Malvolio had just been his usual sleazy self. She'd been sitting on her afternoon break, minding her own business, when he'd come into the coffee room and again suggested they catch up for a drink after work.

Again she'd declined.

'You've got something in your hair.'

He'd come over, had stood behind her where she sat, and, as if being touched by a lizard, she'd flinched as his hand had made contact with her hair. She had screwed her eyes closed as he'd brushed something that surely wasn't there away, wishing the horrible moment over, only the horror hadn't even begun. The lizard had been on the move.

'Come on, Caitlyn…stop teasing me…'

His filthy hands had crept down; she'd been able to hear his breath coming short and hard behind her.

'I'm not teasing you…' Her head had been spinning. The confrontation she'd dreaded—dreaded but convinced herself would never happen, that she was surely imagining things—was actually here. *'Malvolio, you're married…'*

'Antonia….' His hand had moved down. *'She is so wrapped up in herself and the baby. You and I could be so good together….'*

Paralysed, she'd sat, watched his fingers sneaking at the top of her dress, her brain literally frozen. It had been like being stuck in a nightmare, where you couldn't scream. She'd known that by doing nothing she was implying consent…and if she couldn't speak, if she couldn't scream, then there were two other choices that had sprung to her panicked mind: vomit or bite.

Caitlyn had chosen the latter!

She could still hear his screams of rage—hear again the vile torrent of words he'd spat at her as he'd jumped back—and, like a child, she put her hands over her ears, blocked out what he had said to her. She just didn't want to go there right now.

How, Caitlyn begged herself as she resumed her pacing, could he think she'd teased him? She'd gone out of her way to avoid him, though she had felt his unwelcome eyes on her for months now, had done everything possible to avoid... Her eyes shuttered in wretched horror. The consequences of her resignation were starting to hit home. The prospect of going home and telling her mother that she no longer had work... Oh, a chambermaid's wage wasn't going to change the world, but for now at least it meant holding onto her mother's.

A single mother, Helen Bell had done *everything* to provide not just for her daughter, but for her own father. When Caitlyn's grandmother had died, two years after Caitlyn was born, concerned about her father's declining health and mounting financial problems, Helen had moved back to the family home, working several jobs to pay the mortgage and bills and had gradually cleared his debts. It hadn't all been a struggle, though—the home had been a happy one, with Caitlyn's grandfather more than happy to mind his grandchild while Helen worked hard. And in later years, as his health had declined, both Helen and Caitlyn had in turn been more than happy to care for him—nursing him at home right till the end.

Caitlyn's aunt Cheryl had rarely put in an appearance—until after the funeral. Of course the family home Helen had worked so hard to keep and pay for had been left to her. But Cheryl had had it valued—the beachside suburb close to the city was prime real estate now—and Cheryl wanted not only the generous cash sum that her father had bequeathed to her in his will, but half the value of the family home. Egged on by Roxanne and a greedy lawyer, she was moving heaven and earth to ensure that she got it.

'Bloody Roxanne and Aunty Cheryl…' Caitlyn hissed. Why couldn't they just leave them alone?

The ringing of the phone halted her pacing for less than a second. Her mind was so consumed with her own problems that at first she didn't even give it a glance.

She needed work so badly, but here it would be impossible. Lazzaro was hardly going to fire his own brother-in-law. It would be her word against his. And what about Malvolio's poor wife? How—?

The phone resumed its shrill, and irritated now, unable to ignore it, Caitlyn picked it up.

'Lazzaro Ranaldi's phone. This is Caitlyn Bell speaking.'

She didn't notice Lazzaro come in at first, just listened as a rather exasperated female voice demanded that she be put through.

'I'm sorry, Mr Ranaldi isn't in his office right now. But if you'd like to leave your name, as soon as he returns I'll let him know that you called…'

Half turning, she saw him, and was just about to hand the phone over when instinct kicked in somehow. The dash of bitters in the woman's voice was telling Caitlyn that perhaps this was one call Lazzaro might be glad to miss, so instead of handing him the receiver, she grabbed a pen and scribbled down the woman's name. *Lucy.*

She even managed a little smile when he grimaced and shook his head while Lucy vented her spleen down the phone.

'Of course,' Caitlyn said sweetly. 'I'll be sure to let him know.' Replacing the receiver, she turned to her very soon to be ex-boss. 'You're a bastard!'

'Thank you for passing it on.'

'And she knows you're there and just refusing to talk to her.'

'Anything else?'

'Er, that was pretty much it,' Caitlyn lied. Well, she was hardly going to tell him that 'just because he's fabulous in bed, it doesn't make up for the way he's treated me'. Though she did give him a rather edited version of the teary conclusion to the call. 'She'd like you to call her— any time,' Caitlyn emphasised. 'Any time at all! So…' Noticing his empty hands, she raised her eyebrows. 'Where are the forms?'

'In a filing cabinet.' He gave an apologetic grimace. 'Only I'm not sure which one…but I will write you a cheque now…'

'A cheque's not much good to me at this time on a Friday.' She didn't want to stay another second. Another second and she'd start crying; another second and she'd crumple. The brave façade she was wearing so well was seriously falling apart—the hem unravelling along with the seams—so she hitched her bag on her shoulder and headed for the door. 'Just have it all posted to me on Monday.'

'Caitlyn.' His strong voice summoned her back, but she kept on walking. 'Just listen to me for a moment. What if I were to offer you a job as my personal assistant?'

Now, that was enough to stop her in her tracks—only not enough to make her turn around.

'Me?'

Her hand paused as it reached for the handle and Lazzaro spoke on. 'Clearly I need someone, and you have no idea of some of the poor efforts the agency has sent. You handled that call well, you are qualified, and you are clearly…' he gave a slightly uncomfortable cough '…discreet…'

'I can't.'

The words shot out on instinct—her dream job, everything that she'd wished for coming true, and the money, oh, God, the money would make *such* a difference. Only she couldn't do it—just couldn't do it. And bitter, so bitter, was her regret.

'I can't face seeing Malvolio again.' Her voice was shrill, and still she didn't turn around. Her hand was on the door now, but not to open it, more for support. The horrors of the day were finally catching up, the feelings she had denied, had willed herself not to examine until she was safely alone, were making searing contact with her brain now. 'I don't think I could stand to be…'

Silence filled the room. Only it wasn't peaceful. It was that horrible silence of a strangled sob, the thud of reality, that moment when it all catches up and there's nothing that can be done to push it back down—when you can't keep smiling as if you're stupid, when you can't pretend that you don't care and that it didn't really matter that filthy hands had dirtied your life. Yes—in a while she'd no doubt be able to shrug it off; in a while she'd probably put it all into perspective and apportion the correct blame. In a while it wouldn't matter as much as it mattered now.

But right now it mattered.

And it mattered to Lazzaro too.

Seeing her convulse—seeing this proud, strong woman wilt for a second—he found it mattered enough to propel him from his desk, to literally peel her trembling body from the door, to turn her around to face him and hold her. Like some mountain rescuer he reached her on the cliff-edge and tried to imbue her with his warmth.

'I hate him…' She wasn't talking to Lazzaro; he knew that. 'I *hate* him.'

'I know.'

'I'll be okay soon.' She gulped, knowing she would, just confirming it to herself. She was embarrassed now at letting him see her cry, but he held her closer as she started to pull away, and after just a second of protest she let him—let him comfort her, let him hold her as the horror slowly receded, her breathing slowing at just listening to the soothing thud of his heart in his chest.

For Lazzaro there was one inevitable end to holding a woman in his arms. The luxury of having a penthouse suite as your office meant there was a bed just a door away, and as he stared down at lips swollen from nibbling teeth and salty tears, instinct told him to kiss her—to soothe her in the way he soothed women best. Only a deeper instinct prevailed.

Morality—which was usually void—crept in. His kiss was surely not what she needed now.

Only it was.

It felt like for ever that she'd dreamt of being in his arms, but now it had happened Caitlyn found out dreams didn't actually compare. Being held by him was so blissfully consuming, the circle of his arms so strong and safe, that nothing else could invade. She felt the shift in him, felt the shift from comfort to more, and she actually *wanted* him to kiss her, wanted his hands on her to erase the grubby stains Malvolio's had left.

But he didn't. Instead he held her for just a little bit

more, held her close as she assimilated all that had taken place and put it into some sort of order, and when finally he let her go, when finally she could stand alone again, the world was certainly a nicer place than the one she'd left just moments ago.

'Malvolio manages the housekeeping staff. He's rarely in the office and I'm rarely here. The job would involve a lot of travel…' His voice was low, his gaze direct as he told her he hadn't changed his mind.

'But even so…' Caitlyn protested. 'I'd still have to see him sometimes…' Again she shook her head, but she wasn't so certain now. Lazzaro believed her. Lazzaro knew. And he would, she was sure, sort it.

That thought was confirmed when Lazzaro spoke next. 'He will not trouble you at all—I will go and see him and make very sure of it. You do not have to leave.'

'I haven't got any experience…' She was being offered her dream job, a fast-track to what would normally take years to achieve, and even if it was foolhardy to show how woefully inadequate she was for such an esteemed position, really she had no choice.

'You haven't picked up any bad habits, then.' For the first time today she saw him smile, then he gestured to the desk. 'Sit down.'

Formality was welcome.

Formality she could actually deal with.

So she listened as he took her through her new role, blinking at the description of international flights and luxury hotels that would now pepper her existence, at a salary that made her eyes widen, and at the prospect of a life, as Lazzaro strongly pointed out, that would be basically put on hold to accommodate his.

'My time is valuable,' Lazzaro said, and she nodded. 'Take today—I should not be going to Admin to get forms, and nor will you be able to. That is why you too will have an assistant. My former PA has a list of names somewhere, of people who can be put through to me without question, people who first you check and people who, like Lucy, you will have to deal with.' He gave a tight smile. 'At times your work will be menial, and at times it will be downright boring—such as sitting in a car waiting for me. At other times the stress and demands will be intense. Each morning we will go through my day—each week we will plan my schedule. For example, in a couple of weeks we will fly to Rome—'

'I don't speak Italian…'

'Lucky for you then, that nearly all my staff in Rome speak excellent English… Still, if you do decide to remain in this position, that is something you might be wise to address.'

If she decided to remain! Who would be mad enough to leave such a fabulous job?

Lazzaro must have caught the slightly incongruous dart of her eyes.

'I have never had a PA stay for more than a year—that is how long you will be contracted for. Towards the end of your term we will discuss your future. This is an exceptionally demanding role—and, yes, I am an exceptionally demanding boss. I have high standards, a formidable workload, and at some point you will no doubt decide that no amount of money or perks can make up for it.'

'Is that why Jenna left?' Caitlyn asked, because she'd heard that you should find out the reasons any position was vacant. Though when Lazzaro answered she rather wished that she hadn't.

'Jenna had certain demands that I wasn't prepared to meet.'

Like monogamy? Caitlyn was tempted to say, but thankfully she didn't—their private affair had not been so private, given it was she who had changed the sheets!

'At some point,' Lazzaro continued, 'you will want to resume your own life—I accept that. However, a period of working for me will open many doors for you.'

'I just don't get why me, when it's clearly such a demanding role…' Caitlyn's mouth was suddenly dry—she was acutely aware that she was sitting in a chambermaid's dress, suddenly being interviewed for a plum position. 'And though naturally I'd love the opportunity, I just don't understand why you'd just hand it to me. If it's because of what happened with Malvolio—'

'After several unsuccessful interviews, I wasted yet another hour this afternoon attempting to explain to a very boutique recruitment agency my needs,' Lazzaro interrupted. 'Outlining what it was I was looking for in an assistant. Next week I will be paraded with a number of what they consider suitable applicants. I do not necessarily want someone who speaks fluent Italian. I do not want someone who on paper has "excellent interpersonal skills" but in reality cannot read a situation. I want someone who, without being told, writes down the name of a caller they assume might be difficult.' His eyes narrowed thoughtfully as he looked over at her. 'I guess you just know sometimes that you've found the person you're looking for.'

'Quite!' Caitlyn croaked, then coloured up, biting on her

bottom lip, wishing she were hearing that from him somewhere other than in an interview.

'And,' Lazzaro continued, 'I want someone who has the guts to be honest.'

'I *am* honest…' Caitlyn flared.

'Just not with your bank.' He grinned. 'Look, I am not asking you to sign away the rest of your life. I understand that the role is too consuming, too demanding to expect longevity. But most people I interview are using this as a stepping stone—are prepared to work hard for a few months because of the doors it will open. I want someone who is prepared to work hard, full-stop. So when you are thinking of leaving—which you will—I want you to tell me.'

'Okay…' Caitlyn nodded, only she didn't sound very convinced—wasn't convinced at all, in fact, that she would ever leave. Still, maybe this was the way to get over him, she decided, looking at the multitude of positives. Maybe witnessing his legendary bloody nature first hand might just get her to put out the light on the stupid torch she'd been carrying for him.

'Are you in a relationship?'

'Excuse me?' Caitlyn's response was suitably appalled. 'I hardly think that's relevant.'

'But it is,' Lazzaro countered. 'He is going to have to be one very patient man to accept that he's hardly going to see you—that if this goes ahead, as of Monday, I come first!'

'Well, I'm not in a relationship.' Caitlyn sniffed. 'We just broke up.'

'Excellent.' Lazzaro smiled. 'How long were you together?'

'Why? Are you worried I'm going to be crying into my tissues instead of concentrating on you?'

'I'm just curious.' Lazzaro shrugged. 'Given that we're going to be working so closely together, we're going to get to know these things about each other.'

Hardly! Caitlyn choked back the word—she couldn't imagine asking Lazzaro to pass the tissues as she cracked a bar of chocolate and told him that the reason she and Dominic had broken up was because—because… She closed her eyes and cringed. Because of the things she *didn't* do. Because, at the ripe old age of twenty-two, she was still a virgin!

'Purple!' Caitlyn said instead, giving a tight smile at Lazzaro's bemused frown. 'I'm wearing purple knickers, before you ask, and we were together six months. He ended it, but I was actually about to. Is that enough information for you?'

'For now…' He gave her a very lazy smile, and stared at her for the longest time without even attempting to speak. For Caitlyn it was excruciating as she awaited what she knew was about to be a summing up. 'You're very…' he paused before he delivered his verdict '…different.'

'I am.'

'Very interesting…' Lazzaro mused.

'I'm hard bloody work, actually!'

'I like hard work.' Lazzaro grinned, and she nearly shot out of her chair at the look he was giving her. 'Well, I look forward to working with you. That will be all.'

'Not quite.' Caitlyn saw his frown of surprise and she took a deep breath before speaking. 'Generally at the end of an interview the interviewee is asked if she has any questions or anything she'd like to add.'

'Do you?'

'Actually, yes...' Caitlyn hesitated for a second—could absolutely hear the horrified shriek of the little devil that sat on her shoulder as she decided to be up-front. But there was no point in taking this job, no point at all, if one thing wasn't made perfectly clear from the start. She'd heard Lazzaro was a tough and demanding boss, that he had no qualms at all about speaking his mind—loudly on occasion. That she could accept, so long as Lazzaro could accept her. 'I admire the fact that you speak your mind. However...' her blue eyes locked with his '...so do I.'

'I'd already worked that one out,' Lazzaro countered. 'Though stand-up rows with my personal assistant I can do without.'

'Oh, there'll be no stand-up rows.' Caitlyn smiled. 'I'm more professional than that. But, before you formally offer me the position, you should know that I do have a tongue, and one that I'll use if I think I'm being spoken to inappropri-ately—no matter how good the salary, manners cost nothing.'

Lazzaro, though his face never moved a muscle, was actually smothering a smile; listening to Caitlyn was as unique as it was refreshing—almost as if *he* were the one being interviewed for the job.

'So I am to watch what I say?'

'No,' Caitlyn corrected. 'Just don't expect me to hide behind a pot plant till your mood passes.'

'I don't have any pot plants.'

He stared at her thoughtfully for a moment, and for Caitlyn it lasted for ever. She was wondering if she'd blown it, if she was about to kiss her dream job goodbye, but suddenly he smiled—not a wide, generous smile, more a brief upturn of his lips, but for Caitlyn it was wonderful.

'I will see you on Monday at seven-thirty. You will need a suitable wardrobe, of course. I will arrange an account for you—'

'I *have* a suitable wardrobe,' Caitlyn interrupted. 'I don't generally walk around dressed like this.'

'As you wish.' Lazzaro shrugged. 'But I expect smart.'

'You'll get it.'

'I mean *really* smart,' Lazzaro countered—and winced as the phone rang.

'Allow me.' Caitlyn grinned, rolling her eyes as an expensive voice purred out her new nearly boss's name.

'Bonita,' Caitlyn mouthed, expecting him to shake his head, and more than a little miffed when he didn't.

His manicured hand reached for the phone, his voice surprisingly gentle and familiar as he greeted his caller and then asked if she minded holding for a moment.

'You represent me…' Lazzaro continued, but he was distracted now, clearly wanting this meeting over so he could get back to his call. 'My hotels are the best in the world. A high street suit and cheap luggage is not going to—' He saw her colour up, a little pink tinge come to her cheeks, and he reached in his drawer and scribbled down the name of several stores where he held accounts. 'This is not a favour; this is part of your role if you want the job.'

'Tha—' She stopped herself from thanking him. 'Of course.'

But he wasn't listening. His focus was already elsewhere as he waved her away, and even before she'd closed the door behind her she could hear him talking into the phone.

Only, as much as Lazzaro was listening to Bonita, for a moment his mind was still on Caitlyn.

Watching her walk out of his office, Lazzaro knew he had made the right choice—she was smart, capable, and she had enough guts to stand up to him—and she was damned attractive too… His mouth split in a thin smile. He had absolutely no qualms about mixing business with pleasure…and Caitlyn Bell was going to be just that; he knew it.

An absolute pleasure.

CHAPTER THREE

OPPORTUNITY always knocked when one was least expecting it.

But not only was Caitlyn not expecting it—she actually didn't have time for such a once-in-a-lifetime opportunity to come knocking this weekend. She had a wedding to go to tomorrow, which meant she already had a hairdresser's appointment booked, and then the wedding post mortem on Sunday—in fact, she still hadn't even bought a present.

Which left her about two free hours this evening to buy a fabulous executive wardrobe that would see her through not only her new job in Melbourne, but also a quick dash to Rome.

Stepping out onto the street, Caitlyn walked through the crowded city, her head spinning—not just from Lazzaro's job offer, not just because in a matter of an hour or so her whole life had been turned around... She should be walking on air, but instead her legs felt like lead. It felt as if she was walking through mud and, giving in, she leant against a wall for a moment, watching but somehow not watching a tram clattering through the busy street, the spill of suits leaving their offices, eagerly awaiting their weekends. And though it was the last thing she wanted to think about, though there were a million other things she would rather dwell on, it was Malvolio she couldn't rid from her mind.

A nauseous feeling rose in her throat as she relived the horrible scene. Saw again the hate in his eyes when she'd bitten him, heard again the vile spit of words as he'd stormed out of the door.

'You're a cheap slut, Caitlyn—just like Roxanne.'

Roxanne...

Caitlyn closed her eyes, willed her heart to settle into a more normal rhythm. The name he'd hurled meant that he knew who she was—a revelation she hadn't been prepared for.

After ascending the elevator in a city department store, as usual she got off on the fourth floor. It took about ten minutes of blind panic for her to realise that no half-price suit in a sale was going to do for Lazzaro.

He wasn't doing her a favour.

She said Lazzaro's words over and over to herself as she stepped back on the elevator and ascended to the hallowed sixth floor, swallowing at the price tags on the exclusive designer labels, and even accepting the help of a very pushy assistant, whose rather snooty stance noticeably softened when Caitlyn stammered out her predicament.

'*You're* Lazzaro Ranaldi's new personal assistant... So Gemma has left?'

'Jenna.'

'That's right! Jenna shopped here regularly. I know all about how she just *had* to look the part.'

'Really?'

'Your new boss has very exacting standards where his staff are concerned. Absolutely I'll help you.'

Standing in the changing room, Caitlyn stared at her reflection—the safe black suit she'd initially chosen had been tut-tutted away by the assistant and replaced with a slate-grey one, which was gorgeous, a cream linen one, which Caitlyn wasn't sure about, and an olive one which was fab too—although the skirt was just a touch too short for her liking. Now she was wearing a chocolate-brown suit that, as the assistant had promised, did work well with her colouring. It calmed her complexion and brought out the blue of her eyes, and with her hair done, with make-up on and the right shoes… Standing on tiptoe, Caitlyn assumed a snooty pose and decided that she actually might just pass as Lazzaro Ranaldi's assistant—and she could afford to help her mother now, could pay the lawyer and, if the ruling didn't go their way, would be able to pay off Aunty Cheryl and Roxanne.

Roxanne…

Sitting on the bench in the changing room, Caitlyn buried her head in her hands and dragged in the stuffy air. The knot that was so familiar in her stomach these days tightened another notch, as if Roxanne and Cheryl were on either side, pulling, tugging so hard it would be easier sometimes to just let it snap. Their vile conversation was still playing on her mind as clearly as if it had taken place yesterday instead of two years ago. And not for the first time, maybe for the millionth, Caitlyn wondered if there was anything she could have done—anything she could have said—that might have changed the appalling outcome.

They'd gone to Roxanne's on the Sunday—Helen to

plead with Cheryl to please come and visit now and then. Caitlyn and Roxanne had left them to it, taken a bottle of champagne upstairs and attempted a girls' night in.

Attempted—as they had since they'd been little girls— to pretend they were friends.

'What's this?' Roxanne's eyes had lit up as Caitlyn's bag had tipped off the bed, the photo of Lazzaro she'd torn out of a magazine falling on the floor. 'You've got a crush on him, haven't you?'

'No!' Caitlyn had snatched back the picture, her face burning. But an excuse to talk about Lazzaro had been just too impossible to pass up. 'But you should see how he runs the place—he's pretty amazing.'

'He's hot…' Roxanne had grinned. 'I'll give you that.'

Brave or foolish, Caitlyn hadn't been able to help but show off a little bit to her cousin. 'He gave me a lift home last night.'

'You?' Roxanne scoffed. 'He's ferrying the staff home now, is he? Things must be getting tight!' Roxanne stared down at her newly painted toenails. 'I'm sick of the Ranaldis. I thought I was on to a good thing with Luca, and it turns out the guy's a complete loser.'

'Hardly a loser,' Caitlyn countered. 'And if he's anything like his twin then he must be stunning.'

'He's broke,' Roxanne groaned. 'Luca Ranaldi's a drunk, and he's broke.'

'Broke?' Caitlyn frowned. The words 'broke' and 'Ranaldi' didn't exactly belong in the same sentence, but Roxanne just giggled, opening her wardrobe and pulling out dress after dress, then pulling out a box and smiling at Caitlyn's shocked expression over the glittering array of jewels. 'He's bought you all *this?* But I thought you just said he was broke.'

'What salesperson would even think to check *his* credit rating? He's living off his reputation—though not for much longer,' Roxanne said darkly. 'Lazzaro's covering all his rapidly bouncing cheques.'

'So what the hell are you doing, accepting these things?' Caitlyn said hotly. 'Roxanne, if the guy's going under…'

'Then he might as well go under in style. Anyway, a few piddly dresses and some jewels are a drop in the ocean compared to his problems. I was actually going to dump him today, but he said that he'd take me car-shopping on Monday.' She tossed over a few brochures. 'I'm thinking I might go for red.'

'Roxanne!'

'Oh, get a life,' Roxanne snapped. 'Once I've got rid of Luca I intend to.'

'How are you doing? I've got some luggage for you to—' The shop assistant whipped back the curtain, her painted smile wavering as Caitlyn looked up. 'Are you feeling all right?'

'I'm fine.' Caitlyn ran a tongue over dry lips and stood up. 'Just fine.'

They were so in love.

The words taunted her as she stared in the mirror. Aunty Cheryl had said them over and over, her mother too—it had even been in the newspapers, with a photo of Roxanne having to be held up as she walked behind Luca's coffin.

But Caitlyn knew the truth—and it would seem that Malvolio did too.

* * *

'What's happening?' Lazzaro frowned as, not only was the phone picked up at his sister's home, but Antonia herself answered.

'Nothing. Why?'

'I thought you had pains? That you were—'

'Hardly…' Antonia sighed. 'I don't think this baby's ever going to come out. What are you doing?'

'Driving… Is Malvolio there?'

'He's just outside. I'll get him—'

'Don't worry.' Lazzaro interrupted his sister. 'I'll call over—I'm just a few minutes away.'

'Well, stay for dinner. I could—' Antonia started cheerfully, then stopped mid-sentence as the phone cut out—not that she gave it much thought. Her brother Lazzaro wasn't exactly known for his small talk.

Putting down her book and trying to heave herself off the couch, Antonia smiled as the housekeeper opened the front door and her brother strode into the lounge. 'I was just asking if you wanted to stay for dinner before you hung up on me.'

'No…' Lazzaro shook his head.

'Stay,' Antonia insisted, but still he shook his head.

'Zio!' Marianna's squeal was delighted as she padded into the living room, dressed in pink pyjamas and a dressing gown, her dark curls bobbing as she ran delightedly towards him. Normally he scooped her up, rained her fat baby face with kisses—only he couldn't today. He felt sick with indecision as he looked from his sister to his niece, not wanting to be the one to burst their bubble.

'Hey…' Lazzaro ruffled Marianna's hair, tried not to notice the disappointment in the little girl's eyes at his cool greeting. 'It's good to see you, Marianna.' He turned his attention back to his sister. 'I just wanted to have a word with Malvolio—about work…' he added, completely unable to look at her now.

But Antonia wasn't having it, and called to the house-keeper, asking her to take Marianna for a play, before talking to her brother.

'Is everything okay, Lazzaro?' Antonia checked. She hadn't seen Lazzaro as bad as this for ages. Tense, dis-tracted, he was like a coiled spring. 'You seem…'

'I'm just tired,' Lazzaro answered, forcing a smile of his own. 'It's been a busy week. You heard about Jenna leaving?'

'Poor you. Let's hope you get someone soon.'

'I already have.'

'Already? That's quick. Normally it takes you for ever to find someone suitable.'

'Not this time.'

'So stay for dinner,' Antonia pleaded. 'Marianna would be delighted, and so would I—it would help me take my mind off this little one.' She ran a hand over her swollen stomach. 'I'm getting more nervous by the minute.'

'You're going to be fine,' Lazzaro said, and even tried to smile as he did so. 'You're both going to be fine. What are you reading?'

'A baby name book—I'm down to about thirty names for a girl, but if it's a boy…' She paused for a second, watching as Lazzaro swallowed, pain flickering across his usually impassive features. 'I want to call him Luca.'

'That's good.' Lazzaro nodded. 'That's how it should be—it is the right thing to do.'

'You're sure? I mean, I know…' She didn't finish her sentence, waited for Lazzaro to fill in the impossible gap.

Only he didn't, instead running a hand over his forehead, then squeezing the bridge of his nose between his thumb and forefinger for a second.

'Talk to me, Lazzaro.'

'There's nothing to say. I just…' He couldn't even think it, let alone say it, and Antonia tried to help him.

'You think you'll never be able to say that name again without remembering…?'

'I'll always remember,' Lazzaro countered, because he always did. His late brother was a constant and was always on his mind.

'Without feeling pain, then?' Antonia suggested, but still she didn't get it—the pain too was always there.

'Without regret,' Luca said finally. 'I don't think I will ever be able to think about Luca without feeling regret.'

'Please don't say that…' Antonia's eyes filled with tears—not for her dead brother, but for the agony that remained with the living one. The agony that could never, *had* never been fully discussed. And from the shuttering of his eyes, from the shake of his head, Antonia knew that this was as far as Lazzaro was prepared to go. Only it didn't stop her from trying. 'Lazzaro, if Luca's safe, if he's still with us somehow, then he understands why you had to say what you did—and something *had* to be said, Lazzaro. He was out of control.'

'I know that.' Lazzaro nodded, only they both knew it wasn't the point.

Bravely, Antonia continued. 'And I'm sure he's forgiven you for what you did…' She walked over to him, her voice thick with tears as she pleaded for him to listen. 'If it's any help at all, I forgave you too—a long time ago…' She put up her hand to his cheek, to touch the scar there, but he couldn't let her, pushed her hand away. His sister's forgiveness was not what he needed. 'Lazzaro, you have to let it go…'

'I *have* let it go.'

'Oh, but you haven't, Lazzaro. You're hardly here, and you've hardly been in the same room with our mother since it happened.' Her voice was rising, as if she was anticipating him talking over her, anticipating him terminating the conversation, as he always did. 'We have to talk about it.' There was an almost begging note to Antonia's tone. 'This is killing you—I can see that.'

'There is no point going over and over—'

'We haven't been over it *once!*' Antonia sobbed, her every feature, every movement exhausted—not just from her pregnancy, but from the strain of the past two years. 'Since that day at the hospital it has never been discussed, and we need to do that, Lazzaro—with Mamma too. We need to talk. I need to hear—'

'No, Antonia, you don't!' Lazzaro snapped the words out, watched her recoil at his harshness and hated himself for it. But he consoled himself with the truth: Antonia didn't need to know more of what had happened that day, just as she didn't need to know what had happened this day. If somehow he could carry it alone, somehow he could deal with it, keep it from her, then surely it was the right thing to do? But his voice was a touch softer when he spoke next. 'Is talking going to bring him back?'

'You know it's not.'

'Is talking going to change what happened that day?

Change what Luca saw?' He watched her shake her head in regret. 'Then how the hell can it help?'

'Lazzaro, please…' Antonia begged, but she knew it was useless—knew there was no getting through to him tonight—knew that she had no choice other than to let it go.

'Where's Malvolio?'

'He took his drink outside…' Antonia's voice was flat with weary resignation as she wiped her cheek with the back of her hand and tried to resume normality— whatever the hell that was in this family. 'I'll tell him you're here.'

'I'll go and talk to him out there. You rest up.' He waited till she'd lowered herself back onto the sofa, tried to keep his voice normal, to not betray the bile that was churning in his stomach, the fury that was straining to break free, to look, to sound, to act as if he'd just popped over to see his family.

Family!

In a couple of weeks Malvolio and Antonia would have another baby—a brother or sister for Marianna… What was that bastard doing to his sister, to his niece, to the baby that wasn't even born yet?

As he strode out through the French windows, his mind involuntarily went one step further. What had that bastard done to Caitlyn?

Lazzaro didn't plan things—that was what he paid his staff to do. His busy life was a well-oiled machine that left him free to walk into to any meeting, any boardroom, and instinctively take over—no preparation required for his brilliant mind to assess any situation. But he wished he had prepared for now.

He saw his brother-in-law, his colleague, and to this

point his *friend* standing leaning against the stone wall, a sticking plaster on the hand that was holding his glass. Malvolio's eyes were completely unable to meet his, and for a second Lazzaro truly didn't know what to say.

The truth was so damning, so utterly reprehensible, so loaded with consequence, he wanted to dispute it.

Wanted Caitlyn to be wrong—almost *wanted* her to be *lying*.

Only—sick to the stomach—he was sure that she wasn't.

'What did she say?' Malvolio's face was as white as chalk, a muscle pulsing in his cheek. 'What did that little bitch have to say—?'

He never got to finish. He was yanked forward by his jacket a generous few inches, then slammed back hard against the wall.

'Shut it,' Lazzaro snarled, his face inches away from Malvolio's. 'You make me sick.'

'You believe her?' Malvolio gave a nervous but mocking laugh. 'You believe her against your own family?'

'You are married to my sister,' Lazzaro snarled. 'You are not my blood. What the hell are you doing, messing around?'

'I wasn't. She's the one who was coming on to *me*. She's the one who set me up.'

'Rubbish,' Lazzaro snarled. 'Don't try and lie your way out of this. You go near her again and I will not be responsible for my actions.' Lazzaro's hands were still pushing him up against the wall, his voice low and menacing. 'You stay well away from her.'

'You mean you haven't got rid of her?' Malvolio's voice was aghast.

'Why would I get rid of her when it was *your* mistake?

She is my personal assistant now—and one wrong move from you and don't think I won't tell my sister.'

'She set me up.' Malvolio had rallied. 'She's set you up too.'

'What are you talking about? You were the one trying to lure her with talk of a promotion, watching her all the time—and that's not from Caitlyn; that's from another staff member.'

'Lure her!' Malvolio let out an incredulous snort. 'She was the one coming on to *me*, Lazzaro. Now she's got her fancy qualifications she thinks she's entitled to the top job—she wanted to know if, with Jenna gone, I could find an opening for her. She's always after favours—wanting her payslips fiddled. You should have seen her…'

Malvolio raked a hand through his hair, his breathless voice growing stronger with every word as Lazzaro stepped back, shaking his head, refuting it and yet hearing it—hearing and starting to if not believe it, then… His already loosened tie seemed to be choking him, and Lazzaro pulled at his collar, the open-and-shut case that had assured his tirade wavering at the final summing up as Malvolio continued.

'She was all over me. I didn't know what to do—I told her you were interviewing, that I couldn't do her any favours, and the next thing she bit me, screaming that I'd come on to her—'

'You're lying.' Lazzaro snarled the words out. 'Lying to save yourself—because without my family, without your job, without us, you are nothing. Without me propping you up you would be the nothing you were before you met my sister.' He hissed out a curse. 'Why am I protecting

you? She would be better off without you…better off
knowing the truth…'

'No!' Malvolio shouted the word. 'I love Antonia—as
if I'd jeopardise things with a tart like that. As if I'd mess
up the kids' lives like that,' Malvolio went on. 'She was so
upset by me that she had to leave, was she?' He gave an
incredulous laugh. 'Only she wasn't so upset when you
upped her salary. It would seem she can stomach staying
if the price is right. She can't be *that* distressed by me…'

Lazzaro could hear the blood pounding in his temples,
a drench of relief flooding him. Because if Malvolio was
telling the truth then his sister was okay, the kids were okay.
And as for Caitlyn… The shot of relief was temporary. He
knew the pain in her eyes had been real. He was sure. He'd
felt her heart fluttering in her chest when he'd held her.
Lazzaro knew women—knew when he was being lied to—
she couldn't have played him that well.

'You know who she is, don't you?'

Malvolio's voice seemed to be coming from a long way
off, but he didn't get to finish. The French doors were
opening and Antonia was stepping out. Thankfully though,
Lazzaro was saved from faking casual in front of his
sister—as his mobile trilled he left it to Malvolio to make
the small talk and tell her they'd be in soon. It took a
moment to tune his brain into the conversation, as the
clipped voice introduced herself as a saleswoman from a
downtown department store.

'Just to confirm some spending on a new signatory. I
need to run through the purchases, if I may?' And he
listened—listened as designer suits, coats, shoes and boots
were reeled off, listened as he heard how the woman who

had insisted she could manage smart, had actually in less than an hour managed to pretty much top Jenna's annual clothing budget. 'And a full set of Oroton luggage. You're aware of all these purchases?'

'I am.' Lazzaro nodded, more to himself than to the woman on the other end of the line. Jenna had cost a fortune to kit out initially, he recalled. Of course Caitlyn would need coats and boots for Italy. He'd never questioned a bill like that in his life, and he wasn't about to start because of Malvolio.

Turning off the phone, he smiled to his sister as Malvolio assured her they'd be inside in just a moment.

'Everything's okay, isn't it?' Antonia checked nervously.

'Of course.' Lazzaro smiled, but it faded the second his sister was back inside, and the conversation resumed exactly where it had left off, the whole sordid mess of this afternoon taking a darker, sicker twist.

'She's Roxanne's cousin.' Malvolio sneered the words and Lazzaro's face visibly paled.

Caitlyn Bell was Roxanne's cousin.

Roxanne Martin was the person he hated most in the world.

The woman who had pitched brother against brother.

The woman who had so much blood on her hands she might as well have killed Luca with her own bare ones.

'You're the one talking about family,' Malvolio carried on savagely. 'You're the one talking about blood relations. Well, your new personal assistant comes from the same gene pool as Roxanne Martin.'

No!

Lazzaro's brain tightened in denial, the word on the tip

of his taut lips. The woman he had spoken to this evening, the woman he had held in his arms for a short while, was nothing, *nothing* like Roxanne.

But just as he was about to refute it, sense took over. Denial was dangerous.

Denial—the impossible dance that had led Luca to his early grave.

Only he was stronger than Luca.

The eyes that had held his were swimming into his vision—only with dangerous undertones. And though he was initially tempted to ring the store, to cut her credit, to retract his job offer, instead a bitter smile twisted his lips… So what if he'd hired a manipulative, lying, little bitch? It could be worse—he might not have known it!

'You'd better be telling the truth—because if you ever hurt my sister…' Lazzaro pinned his brother-in-law with his eyes, watched as he shrank against the wall. 'If I let you live, it will only be to ensure that you regret it!'

'And Caitlyn?' Malvolio's eyes darted as he voiced the unpalatable question. 'You'll get rid of her? I mean, given what I've told you…'

'Get rid of her? Why would I do that when things are just starting to get interesting?' Lazzaro's dark laugh was mirthless. 'If Caitlyn Bell thinks she can play me then she hasn't done her homework properly. I'm actually looking forward to it.'

CHAPTER FOUR

'IT SAYS here Roberta called.'

His voice held the warning ring that was becoming increasingly familiar. Her first week working for Lazzaro and already she was looking at the clock, willing the next few hours to just please hurry up and go, so that she could wave goodbye to him till Monday.

'She did.' Caitlyn gulped, not looking up, staring instead at the note he had put on her desk—focussing not on the message she'd written but on his tense fingers that were drumming over it. 'Half an hour ago. But you were on another call…'

'And what did you say to her?'

'Just that,' Caitlyn offered. 'I said that you were on another call and I'd let you know…' A rather shaky finger hovered near his and pointed to her note. 'Which I did.'

'She told you it was urgent, I presume?'

'She did.' Caitlyn cleared her throat. 'But nearly everyone—'

'You do realise that I've been trying to get hold of her for two days?' His voice was pure ice.

'She sounded anxious,' Caitlyn attempted. 'She sounded like—'

'She probably *was* anxious, given that I told her that if she didn't get back to me by five p.m. Friday I would be commencing legal proceedings—which I was just in the process of till I saw your little note. Why the hell didn't you think to check? Of all the bloody incompetent—'

'Now, hold on a minute!' Standing up, even in killer heels, she was no match for his height—or his wrath—but she gave it her best shot. He'd been bloody all week— nothing like the man who'd interviewed her—and Caitlyn was seriously wondering if she'd see out the first week, let alone last a year! 'Her name wasn't on Jenna's precious list, and if I put through every anxious, depressed, teary or tipsy woman who calls for you, you might as well get rid of your desk and sit at one of those old-fashioned switchboards! "Mr Ranaldi…"' she mimicked—who, she didn't know, but she was boiling angry now. '"Just connecting you now!"'

'Next time someone you don't know calls for me,' Lazzaro said tartly, but his mouth was actually twitching as he tried not to smile, 'you are to check with me.'

As if on cue her phone rang and, still bristling, Caitlyn picked it up, introducing herself calmly. Just a teeny glint came to her eye. 'One moment, please. I'll just check.'

'Tanya.' She smiled sweetly, but her eyes were mutinous. 'Should I put her through?'

'No!' Lazzaro snapped.

'Only she says it's urgent—she sounds quite anxious, actually!'

'Tell her I've left for the weekend.' He raked a hand through his hair. 'But now you've bloody put her on hold she's going to *know* I'm here!'

'I'm so sorry to keep you waiting.' Taking Tanya off hold, Caitlyn was as sweet as she was convincing. 'I thought I might be able to catch him at Reception for you, but he's already left for the weekend—I'll be sure to let him know that you called, though.'

Replacing the receiver, she waited—would wait till Monday if she had to.

'Okay…' He gave the tiniest shrug. 'Next time just…' His voice trailed off.

'Just what?' Caitlyn pushed. 'Do you want me to put them through, check with you, or use my initiative? Which, given I don't possess psychic powers, isn't always going to be spot-on!'

'Okay! *Okay!*' He threw his hands up in exasperation before storming off. 'I accept that.'

'So do I,' she said to his departing back. 'Your apology, that is.'

And for the first time in the whole week—at five past five on Friday—he smiled. Actually turned to her and smiled.

'You're pushing your luck now! I still have to ring Roberta—*and* call off my lawyer.' But he was still smiling! 'Look, why don't you go home?'

Which was better than an apology, given that every other night she'd been here till well into the double digits. 'Well, if you're sure…' Caitlyn sniffed, still refusing to completely forgive him.

'Of course. You've worked hard this week.' It was the first compliment he'd paid her since she'd started, and all her anger just evaporated. Finally returning his smile, she reached for her bag. 'I'll see you at seven a.m.'

'Seven a.m.?' Caitlyn blinked. 'But it's Saturday tomorrow.'

'Which is exactly why I want to check out the peninsular resort. I'm considering buying it to offer my overseas clients a break from the city at weekends—so naturally I want to spend a weekend there.'

'But it isn't booked,' Caitlyn said hopefully, visions of collapsing in the bath, shaving her legs and putting on a face mask, or just doing nothing, fading as the reality of this job caught up.

'We'll ring on the way.' Lazzaro shrugged. 'I'd like to see what they come up with at short notice, and we'll use an alias—I don't want them to even have a hint that it's me who's arriving.' He registered her frown. 'I'm always one step ahead of everyone, Caitlyn, that's why I'm so successful. You'd do well to remember that.'

And even though he was still smiling, somehow it didn't reach his eyes—somehow, as Caitlyn headed for the door, she felt as if he was warning her.

It wasn't so much a question of juggling her life around her career, Caitlyn thought at seven the next morning, as Jeremy pressed the remote control and the heavy gates opened to Lazzaro's impressive home—working closely with the great Ranaldi there could *be* no life. The role of Lazzaro's PA, as she'd found out in her first week, was an all-consuming one. They either met at the hotel or at his home—whatever his schedule dictated—and, boy, did his schedule dictate. In the week she'd been working for him, Caitlyn had racked up more air miles than she'd had in her entire life up to now. Lazzaro used helicopters the way other people used taxis, and Interstate trips for a two-hour meeting barely merited comment. Waking before sunrise, showering and dressing before Lazzaro's driver collected her, and the draining day began—then she'd crawl into bed, often not before midnight, only to sit bolt-upright as her alarm trilled and the whole exhausting circus started again....

Taking a final gulp of her take-away coffee, and hoping the caffeine would get to work soon, Caitlyn wearily climbed out of the car and, fixing a smile in place, knocked on his heavy front door, wondering what sort of mood she was going to find behind it.

'Good morning!' Used to not getting an answer, Caitlyn pushed it open, her high heels echoing on the floorboards, then silencing whenever she hit one of the thick luxurious rugs. Her new shoes were already starting to hurt as she called out into the empty hallway—this was only the third time she'd been to his home in the morning, and on both other occasions Lazzaro had greeted her from the kitchen with the briefest of good mornings and a rapid rundown of their schedule.

But not this morning.

Feeling like an intruder, she walked along the darkened hallway—the luxurious surrounds were not quite familiar enough yet to fail to impress. His Toorak mansion home had been meticulously decorated, with no expense spared—exquisite antique furniture clashed marvellously with the latest in everything modern—but it was definitely a male home. Feminine touches were markedly absent— no flowers brightening corners, no splashes of colour to take away the rather austere lines, no photos on the heavy wooden furniture to draw the eye.

Glancing into the lounge as she walked past, she saw the usually immaculate room was dishevelled—given the ungodly hour, it hadn't been attended to by the house-keeper—but it was the cushions that were tossed on the floor that had Caitlyn pausing. Like a cat sniffing the air, sensing an intruder, she caught an unwelcome whiff of a heavy, exotic perfume, saw the impressive stereo system flashing like a beacon in the darkness. Presumably he hadn't had time to turn it off before he'd headed to bed. Knowing it shouldn't irk her, but accepting that it did, Caitlyn gave her head a little shake and her mind a little talking-to as she headed into the kitchen.

Get used to it, Caitlyn. Living in Lazzaro's pocket, she was going to have to get used to stumbling on his loose change—oh, and there was plenty: Lucy, Tabitha, Mandy, Tanya… Each name twisted the knife in her stomach a notch as it purred down the phone—and each time Lazzaro refused to take the call it loosened a little. Maybe it was Bonita, Caitlyn thought drily—the woman whose calls he took without question; a woman whose thick, throaty voice could haul Lazzaro out of any meeting.

Caitlyn gave an uncomfortable swallow, wondering if it was Bonita she was about to meet and telling herself she could deal with it—reminding herself that she was his employee, his assistant.

It mustn't matter a jot how she felt about him.

Still, no amount of reminding herself of her place in his life was going to stop it hurting, and as she entered the kitchen Caitlyn tried and simultaneously failed not to notice the empty champagne bottle on the stone bench...tried and failed not to notice the two glasses beside it.

Tried and failed not to notice the lipstick marks on one of the glasses.

For an appalling moment she wondered if she was disturbing something—braced herself as she heard footsteps on the stairwell for the sight of some ravishing, exotic beauty.

But it was only Lazzaro!

Bloody hell! Caitlyn thought, ducking from under the light and hoping the shadows would hide her blush as she busied herself with her briefcase. Couldn't he at least put some clothes on?

Dressed *only* in trousers, the button not even done up, damp from the shower, patting his freshly shaven jaw with a towel, the usually immaculate Lazzaro was unusually untogether—and, though not the one she'd dreaded facing, he was certainly a ravishing, exotic beauty. The swarthy olive skin that so far Caitlyn had only witnessed from the collar up or the cuffs down was blissfully exposed now...

'I'm running late...' Damp jet hair flopped over his forehead, and the musky tang of freshly applied aftershave mingling with damp skin almost asphyxiated her as he brushed past—only it wasn't the scent that was causing her throat to tighten, trapping her breath in her lungs, it was the man wearing it. 'Coffee?'

A simple question—a needless one, almost, as caffeine was the one thing that had got her through the previous week. But though Caitlyn had shared more coffees with him than she could count it seemed different somehow— here in his home—with Lazzaro making it.

'Coffee?' He frowned at her muteness, at her hesitant

blushing nod, then turned his back—which didn't help matters much. She could feel her nails digging into her palms as he stretched up and opened the cupboard above him, the simple movement allowing a teasing glimpse of muscle definition. She *really* wished he'd put some damn clothes on—wished normal services could be resumed. Because with Lazzaro semi-naked in the kitchen, her thought processes scattered like leaves in the wind, and she could only hope he didn't pull out three cups—that Lazzaro's *visitor* wasn't going to be joining them or, worse, that Lazzaro wasn't going to take *her* a drink.

Lucky the woman who woke to him…

The leaves caught in a gust, her thoughts fluttered skywards. She was picturing the heaven of that usually inscrutable face smiling down at her with tenderness upon waking, then feeling that surly mouth awakening her with a lazy kiss.

'Here…' Unlike hers, his hand was completely steady as he handed her a coffee, as he served her a front-row, best seat view of his chest, and she actually couldn't take it from him—just couldn't. She just sat on a kitchen stool and swallowed as he leant over her just a little bit and placed it on the bench behind her, treating her to a generous glimpse of his underarm hair as he stretched. She'd read somewhere that women shouldn't shave there, that underarm hair was just loaded with lusty fragrances that would dizzy your lover if only you dared. Whoever had written it must have been right because, whether Lazzaro was fresh out of the shower or not, something animal was happening—her head was spinning as the air between them seemed to still. His nipple was in her face, and she wanted to lick it. Torrid, unfamiliar thoughts were pinging in—intimate thoughts. This was their morning. She glimpsed her dreams and elaborated them a touch. This was what it could be like each and every morning…

God, but she was gorgeous. A bag of nerves, perhaps, but utterly, utterly gorgeous.

The last week had been difficult in the extreme—with Lazzaro waiting for her to make a mistake, waiting for her to slip up, to show her true colours. Only to date all she had been was a breath of fresh air…clipping in and out of his office with her wide smile, charming his colleagues and the boss to boot! There was no question she was capable of the role—would, in fact, be *extremely* capable once she'd mastered a few more of the basics.

Sometimes he actually forgot for a moment just who she was…

At moments like this one he actually forgot that she was Roxanne's cousin. Lazzaro could see her hands in her lap, her knees bobbing up and down, and he wanted to still them—wanted to trap her legs with his thighs, wanted to take that mouth with his and taste it. Why couldn't he have felt like that last night? Listening to Mandy—or was it Mindy?—droning on and on. As beautiful as she was, he hadn't even been bothered enough to shut her up with a kiss, hadn't even felt a stirring—which for Lazzaro had proved extremely worrying. Rising to *any* occasion had never, ever been an issue—only it would have been last night. Which was why he'd had his driver take Mandy home—why, after a quick drink, he'd pleaded exhaustion.

Lazzaro wasn't tired now, though—in fact he was very, very awake. The air was thick with arousal, and the heat that was burning from her mouth warmed him. Their breathing matched. He could see the curve of her bosom as it rapidly rose and fell, and it actually felt as if they *were* kissing. He could see her tongue bobbing out, rolling over her bottom lip. Both were silent, both just staring, both feeling it—an *it* that was impossible to deny—this bit of ice that reared between them now and then. Ice that really needed to be broken…

'Should we just go upstairs? Get it over with…?' His voice was low and gruff, his eyes smiling down at hers.

If anyone else, under any other circumstance, had said that, she'd have died. But she actually laughed, grateful that he'd acknowledged it, made a sort of joke about it, so that she could too.

'Only I don't think I can walk about like this all day— it would be extremely uncomfortable!'

'Well, you'd better get used to it,' Caitlyn retorted. 'Because I've seen your schedule and we certainly haven't got time for any of that nonsense—anyway, I've just done my make-up.'

He laughed, and amazingly she wasn't blushing any more. In fact, Caitlyn realised, she was flirting—she, Caitlyn Bell, the last virgin on earth, the most unskilled flirter alive, was actually teasing the sexiest man of them all. And she was doing it rather well, she realised, as he actually pushed just a little bit harder, and she actually glimpsed a note of regret when he smiled and winked.

'Pity!'

Now she *could* pick up her cup, and she took a drink.

'Pity,' he said again. 'It would have been marvellous, you know!'

Skimming the newspaper as they left the city behind, still he managed to dish out his orders.

'Book a massage for you—all the best treatments—and book golf for me. Tell them I need to hire everything,' Lazzaro prompted as she pulled out her phone.

'Women do play golf too,' Caitlyn responded tartly as she dialled the number. 'Some rather well…'

'Fine.' Lazzaro bared his teeth in a smile. 'You play golf, if you prefer—I could use a massage, actually!'

Given the only thing Caitlyn knew about golf was that it sounded boring, she made reservations for 'Mr Holland' and his assistant Miss Bell, blushing as she did so. Definitely *not* refusing to give in, she ordered a few rather luxurious-sounding treatments for herself.

'Not much of an alias,' Lazzaro drawled as she clicked the phone off.

'I'm not the one with anything to hide,' Caitlyn teased back. But he mustn't have got her sense of humour, or something must have been lost in translation, because instead of smirking back at her, as she'd expected, his face hardened, his eyes narrowing for a moment, staring at her as he had all last week.

Looking at her as if he didn't even like her.

The mobile ringing in his pocket went unanswered, Lazzaro instead flicking his eyes away and staring moodily out of the window. The sun was rising on an already warm day, hitting the high-rise towers of the city, and despite the air-conditioned car, Caitlyn felt drained. Even after the strong shot of coffee, Caitlyn suddenly felt weary—the teasing fun they'd had this morning but a distant memory now. It was clearly going to be another very long day.

'Caitlyn Bell.' When her own mobile rang she answered without checking—glad for the diversion, actually, with Lazzaro suddenly in this black mood. 'Oh, Antonia,' she said, and Lazzaro looked over sharply. 'How are you?'

'Today's the day…' Caitlyn could hear the excitement laced with fear in his sister's voice. 'We're on our way to the hospital now. I've tried to get hold of Lazzaro at home, and on his mobile—he's not with you, is he?'

Caitlyn was saved from having to answer by Lazzaro giving a rather irritated sigh and snapping his fingers for her to hand over the phone. But when he spoke to his sister his voice was light and easy—though Caitlyn couldn't help but notice every bit of his body language said otherwise.

'How are you?' Lazzaro greeted his sister. 'That's fantastic!' He paused and laughed. 'Well, don't be—you know they say the second labour's always much easier.'

Since when was Lazzaro such an expert on childbirth? Caitlyn thought, irritated. But clearly Antonia, in her present state, had no trouble voicing it!

'You should know by now that I'm an expert on *every-thing*!' Lazzaro responded. 'I thought you weren't due for another week.' His fingers were tapping on his thigh as Antonia answered. 'It's just bad timing at this end—I can't cancel this weekend. It's been booked for ages.'

And Caitlyn watched—watched as he lied through his very white teeth, and didn't even blush as he proceeded to lie a whole lot more.

'I wish I could, Antonia, but there's nothing I can do about it. You are to let me know the second there's news. Good luck!'

Clicking off the phone, he handed it back to Caitlyn without a word—then turned again to the window as Caitlyn's mind whirred like a merry-go-round. Oh, she'd heard Lazzaro lie to women—had lied to them on his behalf on more than a couple of occasions—but what she couldn't fathom, what she was having trouble comprehending, was that he'd lie to his own sister. A sister who, over the past week or so, Caitlyn had spoken to. A sister he seemed genuinely fond of—*his* sister, who was clearly in labour.

He didn't have to cancel this trip—they hadn't even been expecting him!

Lazzaro could sense her disapproval, and for once it unnerved him—though his assistant's approval was usually the last thing he required as he got on with the business of being a Ranaldi. Yet he was tempted to tap Jeremy on the shoulder and tell him to stop the car and let him out. He wanted out of the car and away from the bloody lot of them.

Tapping his fingers impatiently, Lazzaro dismissed the odd impulse. He didn't really want to be alone with his thoughts today of all days. It wasn't Caitlyn's disapproval that was gnawing at him—it was his own dread and loathing.

He was trying to centre himself. It was as if he was surrounded by a million scattered compasses, and the needles which had hovered without direction for so long were suddenly settling, all homing in as the universe moved the world along, as everything aligned to bring things to an unwelcome head. A new life was coming into the world—a new life that meant his shattered family would have to meet, might talk…

That he might have to face the dead.

CHAPTER FIVE

THE entire day was to be exhausting.

Oh, the resort was fabulous—as they swept up the pebbled drive the lush green of the golf course was a rare sight after the long drought-filled summer. Water was spraying into the sun, and on appearance alone the temperature seemed surely to have dropped a few welcome degrees.

Before his sister's telephone call, when Lazzaro had been capable of talking in more than single syllables, he'd explained that a lot of his overseas clients tired of the city and hotel life—no matter how luxurious—and often went away for the weekends. Lazzaro had shrugged. Why not ensure that their spending money went straight into *his* account?

The building was cool and welcoming as they entered—understated, yet utterly luxurious—and from the second they set foot into the cool, pale lobby, and were then shown to their luxury suites, Caitlyn could see why he wanted it!

Glancing at the vast white bed, it was all Caitlyn could do not to peel off her shoes and just collapse on top. She felt as if she'd worked a full day and it wasn't even nine o'clock! Still, there was no time to feel sorry for herself.

Brimming with energy, Lazzaro tapped on her door about eight and a half seconds later and set her to work.

If Caitlyn thought she'd seen him in action before, today he was absolutely formidable—interviewing key staff as Caitlyn took copious notes, scanning the books as the accountant coughed and fiddled under Lazzaro's very direct line of questioning. Even lunch wasn't relaxing. They'd barely been seated when Lazzaro took an impromptu tour of the kitchen, and then proceeded to order the one thing on the menu that wasn't available.

'You look pleased with yourself.'

'I am…' Lazzaro responded, swirling an asparagus head in butter, then popping it in his mouth. 'Because, despite appearances, this place needs a lot of work.'

'But it's divine,' Caitlyn countered.

'It will be,' Lazzaro affirmed. 'But I've managed to knock at least a couple of zeros off the asking price—they need to sell, and fast.'

'How do you know?'

'Because it's my job to know. Today has been extremely worthwhile.'

'Good.' Caitlyn concentrated on her food as she spoke. 'So, does that mean we'll finish up soon?'

'Why? Do you have plans tonight?'

'No, but you might.' Forcing herself, she looked up at him. 'We've got a lot of work done today. If we push on, maybe we can head back to Melbourne, and you could—'

'Have you any idea how much this place is worth?' Lazzaro interrupted, and though the figure he gave was impressive, Caitlyn remained tight-lipped. 'I am hardly likely to make such a decision before I have seen more of the resort's workings myself. Anyway—' he tried to lighten the tone '—you have a massage booked, and I really should wander over to the golf course.'

'I can't really picture you as a golfer.'

'I'm not.' Lazzaro gave a small unworried shrug.

'You can't just bluff your way through a game of golf.'

'Bluff?' Lazzaro frowned.

'Pretend you're good…' Caitlyn attempted.

'Ahh, but I'm *very* good,' Lazzaro said, standing up. 'I just hate the bloody game—it's not my fault I'm excellent at it.'

There certainly were perks to being Lazzaro Ranaldi's assistant, Caitlyn thought as she lay down on the massage table. Having been exfoliated practically to the bone, and peeled, tweezed and waxed till there wasn't a superfluous hair or skin cell left on her body, it was time for the skilled hands of the masseur to massage away all her tension. Closing her eyes, she tried to relax, tried to close her mind to the jumble of thoughts—and it did help. But only for a little while. Because just as she was almost relaxed, just as she was about to sink into mindless oblivion, it was as if two hands dived in and pulled her up, forcing her to the surface, back to the constant whirl of her thoughts.

When finally she was wrapped in a fluffy robe, sipping a ginger, camomile and lemon tea in her room, Caitlyn honestly wondered if she had the strength to face Lazzaro at dinner tonight. The man whose company she had craved for two years was just too exhausting, too bewildering for her today.

Maybe she could ring in sick?

No such luck. Her phone trilled and, glancing at the caller ID, Caitlyn knew she was going to have to face him.

'Hi, Antonia!' Caitlyn said warmly. 'How are you?'

'Great…though I really wanted to talk with Lazzaro. I'm having no luck getting him on his mobile, and his room phone just keeps ringing out.'

'He's playing golf,' Caitlyn said helpfully. 'He probably didn't take his phone…' Hearing the sigh on the other end of the line, imagining how *she'd* feel if she had such a massive piece of news to share, Caitlyn relented. 'I'll go and knock on his door, and if he's not there I'll pop a note under.'

As she opened her door to do just that, Caitlyn jumped with nerves. The man himself was striding past, frowning as she called out to him— 'It's Antonia…' Slinking back into her room, embarrassed and awkward, Caitlyn sat down and sipped at her disgusting tea as Lazzaro took the call— the call he'd clearly been dreading.

'Fantastic…' For once Lazzaro's usually clipped voice was effusive. 'You've already told her? She must be thrilled!'

If Caitlyn closed her eyes, if she just listened to his words, she'd believe him—could almost envision him pumping a fist into the air at the joyous news. Only Caitlyn's eyes weren't closed, and she could see Lazzaro—leaning against the wall, his shoulders hunched, his forehead resting in the palm of his hand, his profile rigid, a muscle flickering in his cheek as he took in the 'happy' news.

'I'm sorry, Antonia—it's just one thing after another. We're stuck here tonight and most of tomorrow. You should be with Malvolio anyway… Well, I am *buying* this golf course—it seems prudent that I at least give it a go. But I'll be there as soon as I can, and I'll let…'

Caitlyn watched as his free hand bunched into a fist, saw

the little bit of colour that was left in him literally drain away. His Adam's apple bobbed a couple of times before he managed to carry on. 'How was Mum?' He closed his eyes on the excited chatter, raked his hand through his hair and dragged in vital oxygen.

'Of course I hope to see them. It just depends on when we go to Rome... I'm glad you're calling him that—no, really. I'm fine with it now...'

Just for a second his voice broke, and so evident was his pain, so abject his misery, Caitlyn had to force herself not to go over—had to literally stop herself from walking over and taking the phone from his hand, telling Antonia he would call back later.

But Lazzaro recovered quickly, nodding blindly and forcing himself to go on, his cheery voice absolutely belying his hopeless stance. 'Luca would be very proud.'

'A boy?' He didn't look over, just clicked off the phone and stared out of the window into the darkening night. She rued answering the phone—rued that he had taken the call in front of her. She knew, just knew, that this was a side to Lazzaro that he had never wanted her to see.

'They've called him Luca.'

Normally congratulations would be in order. Everything told her they weren't here.

'After my brother...my twin...' He turned just enough to look at her, his eyes holding hers, accusing, almost, and suddenly Caitlyn was nervous. 'Did you ever meet him?'

'How would I have met Luca?' Caitlyn croaked, with no idea why she was blushing guiltily when she hadn't done anything wrong, why he was staring at her as if she had.

'When you were doing work experience, of course.'

Lazzaro's eyes narrowed. 'When did you think I was re-ferring to?'

Did he know Roxanne was her cousin? Caitlyn could feel the sweat beading on her forehead, and despite the massage that had practically rendered her unconscious, and despite a scalp soaked with lavender oil, every muscle in her body was taut with tension.

'I don't know...' She attempted a shrug. 'But, no, I never ran into him. Look, do you want me to book trans-port?' She was attempting normal, attempting professional, trying to do what a good personal assistant would in these circumstances. 'If we get the helicopter—'

'Tomorrow.' Luca shook his head. 'There is too much to do here.'

He didn't elaborate—because, Caitlyn realised, he couldn't. The lies he'd told Antonia didn't match with the truth—and now she knew for sure that today wasn't about sampling the delicacies that would be on offer to his elite patrons. Today served one purpose and one purpose only.

Escape.

And that was reinforced when Lazzaro snapped back into business mode, demanding that she pull out her planner and, despite her rather inappropriate attire, pro-ceeded to go through his schedule.

'We are supposed to be flying to Rome next week. Rearrange things—tomorrow would be better.'

'But what about your sister?' Caitlyn asked. 'Don't you want to arrange some time so that you can see—'

'I do not need you to organise my private life—that I can take care of myself,' Lazzaro interrupted. 'Could you arrange a gift for the baby—and of course flowers...'

'You want *me* to buy your nephew's gift?' Caitlyn tried to keep the slightly ironic note from her voice. *This* from a man who almost in the same breath had told her he could handle his own private life? 'Do you have any idea what you'd like to get him?'

'None,' Lazzaro snapped. 'That will be all.'

As he stood to go, she halted him. 'Lazzaro, can I—?'

'Make a suggestion?' he sneered. 'Are you going to suggest that perhaps I should shop for my own nephew? Or that I should delay going to Rome so that I can spend some time with my family? You know, I really do *not* need to hear your advice, Caitlyn.'

'I wasn't about to give it,' Caitlyn said evenly. 'I was just going to ask if I could have my phone.'

Every question that had flashed into her mind, every question she would never have considered voicing, Lazzaro had just answered—and seeing this proud, strong man look awkward, even for a moment, seeing embarrassment actually taint his features as he offered her her phone, Caitlyn wished she knew him well enough to ask them— wished somehow she could help him.

'I know it must seem…' His voice trailed off, his voluntary attempt at explanation fading before it began. 'You just don't understand.'

'I know I don't.' They were both holding the phone, both holding onto this inanimate object, both staring at it, both looking at it—neither letting go. Behind the strength of his voice she could hear the pain. Behind the terseness she could hear fear. 'I wish I could say the right thing.'

'You can't.' Letting go of the phone, he dragged his fingers through his hair. She half expected him to walk out without another word—could feel the tension in him, the indecision, and nodded when he asked if he could use her bathroom.

He felt sick as he went over and over the conversation with Antonia. He hoped to God he'd sounded happy enough about the news. His mother would soon be on her way—with her latest boyfriend on her arm, no doubt. Running the tap, he splashed water on his face, then did it again, taking in the lipsticks and perfumes that adorned the surfaces. It was easier to focus on nothing than what was in his head. Contraceptive pills, toothpaste—ordinary things, just so out of place in this strange, strange moment.

Baby Luca was here, bearing the name that drenched him in sweat each night, filled his nightmares. The name that he choked on was one he'd have to say daily now… He could see the beads of sweat on his grey complexion—could feel the bile rising within him, no matter how many times he washed his face. God, should he cancel dinner? For the first time he truly didn't know if he could manage normal for an evening—yet at the same time he didn't want to be alone.

'I wish I could help.' She was standing at the open bathroom door, walking in behind him, staring at his reflection in the mirror. And he stared back at her—infinitely better than staring at his own face—so much easier to focus on her beauty than deal with his own demons.

For a moment she'd seemed bold—but as he turned around to her, suddenly she was shy. Lazzaro lifted her chin with his fingers—staring down at her when, as if opening the lid on a velvet box, her eyelashes lifted to show two brilliant sapphires…entrancing, dazzling… bewitching.

The same eyes as Roxanne's. The shade of blue identical. Hell, sometimes he forgot, actually *forgot* that she was using him—actually *forgot* his conversation with Malvolio, actually *forgot* that she'd lied and schemed her way into his life. She was probably lying and scheming right now—right now, at this very minute—trying to worm her way into his heart, trying to get inside his head. Right now, when it was so hard, so very hard to be alone.

When Luca had died he'd sworn never to let a woman get close—never to let a woman under his skin in the way his brother had. But, staring at Caitlyn, blinded by her beauty, it was scarily easy to renegotiate with himself; so very tempting to take the comfort he needed now, to lose himself in the urges he had been resisting since the moment she'd stepped back into his life.

They *were* the same shade of blue—only he could see a swirl of black around each iris that intrigued him. He'd never stared into Roxanne's eyes like this—had never been lulled into the dizzy whirlpool of attraction with Roxanne, never wanted to lower his head to hers the way he did now, towards Caitlyn's...

Only he'd sworn that he wouldn't.

Supremely focussed, incredibly driven, self-control was something he had never had to knowingly exert. He worked hard and, when time allowed, he had the funds and the stamina to play equally hard. His dark good-looks ensured an endless *smorgasbord* of suitable playmates, and his conscience was rarely if ever pricked.

He never promised anything of himself.

So why the dilemma? Why, when never had he craved oblivion more, was he hesitating?

She did something to him—altered his usually direct

thought processes until they were scattered to the wind. Her image darted into his mind's eye over and over throughout the day, and her scent reached him even when she wasn't present—overwhelming him, just as Roxanne had Luca.

This was a woman who *could* get under his skin.

His lips were so close that if she moved a mere inch they would be touching. Only still he hesitated. Still he wrestled with something deep inside. And if life was a series of choices, in that split second Lazzaro's was made: he *would* lose himself in her, *would* drown in the balmy oblivion of lovemaking, *would* bathe in the warmth of her body—only on his terms. He knew he was strong enough to hold back, to take only what he needed tonight and nothing more.

'I don't bite.'

Foolish words, perhaps, but they actually made things easier for him, reminded him of the woman he was dealing with. No matter how sweet her exterior, inside she was as hard as nails—would use him as a means to an end.

Just as he would now use her.

'Oh, but you do!' A smudge of a smile relaxed his lips, but it didn't soften his eyes.

His mouth moved that last delicious fraction, and it was Caitlyn's eyes closing. The bliss of flesh on flesh, of his lips finally on hers—the moment she had dreamed of for so, so long was actually eventuating… His hands were on her shoulders, his mouth moving with hers, and if ever there was a textbook kiss then this was one. His lips were tender, measured, skilled, his tongue sliding around hers… Only as perfect as it might be, even if there wasn't one single thing she could fault, the best Caitlyn could come up with as his mouth moved over hers was that it wasn't *her* perfect.

Dreams were dangerous. Dreams let you inhabit a world that didn't exist—let you savour and taste what you'd never had, what didn't or couldn't exist. Because, as adept and as proficient as his kiss was, no matter how she tried to go with it, no matter how she closed her eyes and attempted to relish this moment, the reality of it didn't match up to her dreams.

'Lazzaro…' She pulled back, shook her head, knowing perhaps she would appear a tease—might in that contrary moment be giving credence to Malvolio's vile accusations—only she couldn't pretend. Couldn't just go along with something that wasn't okay. 'This isn't…'

He felt her detachment before she pulled back. Knew he had lost her before she had gone. But just the taste of her, the smell of her, the feel of her, had him hungry—hungry for all of her. A fierce need was coursing through him, every nerve in his body shrilling demands that their master must not deny them now. And he could do it, Lazzaro said to himself, as he pulled her back in and lowered his head again. He *was* strong enough, Lazzaro told himself—he *could* give just a little bit more of himself and *then* detach.

One hand snaked around her waist, finding the small of her back and wrenching her in as the other knotted into her thick blonde hair, holding her head till there was nowhere else she could go. Kissing her, kissing her as she should be kissed, as he'd wanted to kiss her from the second he'd laid eyes on her, his tongue devoured her, tasted her, drank from her.

His chin was hard on hers, scratching at her skin, his body not just warm but hot through her bathrobe. She could feel herself sink into him, melt into him. His kiss, *this* kiss, was all she had ever imagined—all it should be.

He smothered her—smothered her with rough, urgent, hot kisses that burnt somewhere deep inside, that offered only temporary satisfaction. Every taste made her hungry for more. His hands were on her bottom, wedging her groin into his in an almost needless gesture because she was pressing herself against him too. She closed her eyes as his mouth kissed her hairline, her eyelids, almost bleating with pleasure, with fear, as his tongue explored the hollows of her neck. This time when she pulled back it was for a very different reason—stupidity and inexperience were two different things entirely, and Caitlyn knew exactly where this was going. Knew because her body was telling her—knew that for the first time it felt absolutely right—that this was what to date her lovers' kisses had been missing. And she knew he needed to know.

'I haven't done this before…'

His mouth was still on her neck, kissing her deeply and making her head roll.

'Done what?'

She could feel the warmth of his words on her neck, and the warmth of her blush spread down to greet them as she told him her truth.

'This.'

'What?'

He wasn't kissing her now. Standing to his full height, he was staring down at her, taking in the blonde dishevelled hair. The oil from the massage made it look wet—as if she'd just stepped out of the shower. Her face was flushed, as if the water had been too warm, and her gown had parted just enough to reveal one soft bosom that he wanted so badly to taste.

'I've never made love before.'

Did she think he was *that* stupid?

China-blue eyes stared up at him. That full mouth was quivering with nerves, waiting to be kissed some more, and he was tempted to silence her with just that. What the hell was she playing at? He'd seen her pills in the bathroom, for God's sake, and she'd told him that she'd just broken up with her boyfriend of six months—now she was telling him she was a virgin?

Please!

A very scathing remark was on the tip of his tongue— whatever game she was playing with him was about to be abruptly concluded. The muscles in his arms tensed as he prepared to push her away—only he didn't.

If she wanted to play virgin, if she wanted to pretend that he was her first, then who was he to stop her? In fact, somehow it made it easier to just block out the whys and hows—easier to lower his mouth to hers, to play whatever game it was that she was playing and lose himself.

Pulling her back towards him, Lazzaro kissed the shell of her ear as he spoke. 'Then we'd better take things slowly!'

So slowly. The weight of his mouth on hers was less urgent now, more a slow, languorous kiss, as intimate as it was passionate, exciting her even while simultaneously calming her, telling Caitlyn there was no hurry, no rush on this journey. So she took the time he allowed to explore him—inhaling him, inhaling the undertones of his cologne that couldn't mask the masculine smell of want, feeling the scratch of his face against her skin, coarse, bruising, delicious, and then, because she knew where it was going, because there was nothing to stop her now, allowing herself to concentrate on the blissful feel of his tongue against hers. It toyed with hers, stroking not just where flesh met flesh, but somewhere deeper inside, stirring her slowly, and the weighty band of arousal around her groin danced to the puppet strings he pulled with his mouth.

Lazzaro's hands slipped inside her gown, emitting a groan in their entwined mouths as he encountered the silken smooth, heavily oiled weight of her breasts. He held them in the palms of his hands like ripe fruit, then rolled her nipples between his fingers. Her robe fell in a puddle as he lowered her on the bed, his mouth working its way steadily downwards, and Caitlyn felt her heart still in her throat with nervousness, then trip back into life as she momentarily relaxed, remembering that she had her panties on.

Lazzaro was in no hurry to remove them, but he was kissing her stomach as thoroughly as he'd kissed her mouth, and as his tongue slid down his fingers toyed with her panties, then stopped. She almost sobbed at what was to come. The tease of his tongue through the fabric, the scratch of his jaw high between her legs, the nibble of teeth on lace had Caitlyn squirming with want in his skilful hands as his tongue worked on. But she couldn't relax, couldn't let go and enjoy, because if he didn't stop soon… She could feel her breath catching in her throat, panic building inside. Because if he didn't relent, didn't give her just a second to gather herself…

Her hands were pushing his shoulders, only Lazzaro wasn't letting her go. His shoulders were immovable against the pressure of her hands. *His* hands were stronger as he cupped her bottom and pressed her engorged flesh harder against his mouth. His tongue was inside her panties now, his lips pressed against her, tasting her, drinking her, frenzying her—and her own imagination had been a woeful substitute for reality. The glimpses of satisfaction she had soothed herself with were nothing, *nothing* compared to this. On and ever on he pushed her, and her throat was constricting, stifling her pleas, a sob was catching in her throat.

'Don't…' He whispered the command, and for a second he paused, for a second he looked up…

Fleetingly she asked the question in her jumbled mind—don't what?—but as he dived back down, as his mouth pushed aside her soaking knickers, as his tongue hit her delicious tender spot, she gave herself up to the pleasure of her flesh, her thighs tightening, her bottom arching to his hungry mouth. Her hands were not on his shoulders now, but knotting into his hair. Her intimate lips were kissing him back with a hungry beat that he savoured, in an orgasm that went on for ever, made her almost want to beg for it to stop, and when it was over—when all she wanted to do was curl up her legs and recover—he leant back, smiling down at her as she slowly came to.

'Right…' His voice and his breathing were completely even, his expression utterly deadpan, but there was a glint in his eyes that was almost dangerous as he took in her dishevelled state. 'Let's get started, then…'

Bloody hell! It was the only thing that came to mind as his low voice directed her to the front of the queue for a rollercoaster ride. She'd just had the most amazing orgasm of her life, and Lazzaro hadn't even taken off his top!

God, she was gorgeous… A considerate lover, Lazzaro took pleasure in pleasuring—not out of any sense of duty, more because he loved women, loved feeling them come alive, giving in under his hands, his lips. Only with Caitlyn there *was* a measure of selfishness in his seemingly generous actions—the sweet scent of her skin, the taste of her on his tongue, the moans of pleasure from her throat, had Lazzaro precariously close to ruining his rather formidable reputation.

Lowering himself on the bed beside her, his mouth on hers, feeling her tentative hands running over his chest as they kissed, exploring him, moving with feather-light strokes downwards, Lazzaro knew he wouldn't last a second once inside her. And he so badly wanted to be inside her. His tongue was on her neck now, his lips sucking the tender flesh as his hand moved down to where his mouth had been. His palm held her warm mound as he slipped his finger into her wet, warm space. Biting into her neck, he felt her pleasure as his, felt her moisten beneath him. His erection was dragging on her thigh, nudging its way homeward, hovering there, teasing her, massaging her, tempting her, till it was Caitlyn who had no restraint.

Caitlyn guided that first delicious stab, and then it was Lazzaro, sliding a little way in, then pulling back, staring into her eyes as he did so, monitoring her reaction, tempting her with just a little bit more till her body begged. With each motion her body accommodated this new sensation; with each measured, controlled thrust he held back just enough to make her want more—until she wanted him all: the weight of him on top of her, the feel of him deep inside her, giddying her. Every nerve in her body was fighting the pleasure—because some pleasures were just too great. The control she had lived by, had *had* to live by this past week, was very close to abandonment now.

'Don't.'

He said it again as she fought with herself—said what he had before, the word short and stilted. She could see his shoulders above her, looked down to where he was sliding within, and it was the most erotic thing she had ever seen, the shadowed length of him moving inside her. Only this time he finished what he was saying as a scream curled from her.

'Don't—hold—back.'

'Like you do?' Caitlyn gasped, staring into those black pools and holding them. Because he couldn't ask for all of her without giving all of himself too—and she could feel his restraint, even though it was bliss.

Their eyes locked as they came together, each contraction, each pulse spasmed, and her body squeezed out a scream, her nails digging into his taut shoulders, her mouth sucking on his salty chest as she felt him bucking inside her, felt Lazzaro shuddering his release, their bodies damp, sliding against each other...

'What do you do to me...?' He was still coming, and so was she, and it almost hurt to give so much. She almost hated him for the response he so easily elicited, hated him for making her want him so, for being the one man she wasn't able to resist.

'I told you...'

They were lying in bed. Lazzaro was playing with her hair and Caitlyn was wondering if he was about to get up and leave when his rich voice reached her.

'I told you this morning it would be marvellous.'

Was it? She wanted to check. *Or are you just saying that?* Oh, it had been marvellous for her, but the thought of the beauties he had bedded before was doing nothing for her confidence right now.

She did her best to manage a sophisticated smile as she answered him. 'You did too!' Only she couldn't keep up the charade for long. 'So, what happens now?' Frantic eyes turned to him. 'I mean, it's not very professional…'

'Says who?'

'Says everyone.'

'You only listen to me. I'm the boss; I make the rules.' He realised his words had done nothing to soothe her. 'We'll just be discreet. Obviously we can't make it public—you are my PA, and it would make things awkward on so many levels if people knew that we were…'

He didn't finish. She wished that he would. Were *what?* Caitlyn wanted to ask, only she didn't have the courage.

'Just be discreet.' He kissed the tip of her nose. 'Now, go to sleep…'

He was holding her, still holding her, and she waited, turned her face away from him, waited for him to pull back the rumpled sheets and get dressed and go.

She couldn't bear it for a second longer. 'Are you staying?'

'Why—do you have other plans?'

'It's just that…' She blinked up at the ceiling, her thoughts tumbling out as he smiled and watched. 'Well, actually I'm starving. And I've promised myself that I'll fall asleep every night with my headphones on… I'm doing this crash course in Italian…'

He halted her by leaning over and picking up the phone. And though he cursed at the state of the after-hours menu, never had a club sandwich and icy champagne in bed tasted so good…

Later, Caitlyn reflected. Who needed headphones when she had her very own personal tutor? Her very own Latin lover, whispering in her ear throughout the night and teaching her words that she was sure wouldn't go down too well at any meeting….

CHAPTER SIX

HE WAS very nice to wake up to.

Not that they'd done much sleeping... Caitlyn's inexperience was a distant memory by morning, as Lazzaro had delightedly given her a crash course in lovemaking. A very intensive course in lovemaking, in fact—and she was a very willing pupil, utterly devouring her new-found knowledge and incredibly keen to utilise it!

But lying there, watching him sleeping—watching that normally severe face, that tense body, for once relaxed beside her—she thought that never had he looked more beautiful. His scar just added mystery, though it confused her in some ways. He was hardly vain—Lazzaro took about two minutes to shower and get ready—but for a man who had the best of everything, surely he could have had it seen to...? Caitlyn stared closely at the jagged edges. She could see where the sutures had been placed, and she was so tempted to reach out and touch it, to touch his pain and somehow kiss it better.

As his phone rang, black eyes opened on blue smiling ones.

'Morning...' She reached over to kiss him, unabashed

after last night's intimacies—although if her lack of experience in lovemaking had been taken care of, she was a complete novice in other areas. She had trusted him last night and assumed she could trust him this morning—she had given him her heart and, having fallen asleep in his arms, had never considered it would be handed back in the light of morning.

'Let me see who it is...'

Caitlyn could already see—*Bonita* was flashing up on his caller ID. Her only solace was that he chose not to answer.

'We should get going.' He didn't kiss her back—didn't even try to pretend for a second. Just peeled back the sheets and climbed out of the warm bed. 'I'll meet you downstairs for breakfast.'

'Lazzaro?' She watched his shoulders stiffen at the question in her voice—and knew, because it was indisputable now, that the intimacies they had shared last night didn't extend into the day. Learning fast, and hating the game she found herself playing, Caitlyn checked the slightly needy note in her voice. 'I'll be down in twenty minutes.'

He was far bolder than she could ever be. He didn't even attempt to pull on yesterday's grubby clothes, just wrapped a towel round his waist and picked up his things before heading off to his own room to get showered and dressed, leaving Caitlyn blowing her fringe skywards as she lay on the bed, trying not to cry—determined not to give him the satisfaction of her tears.

Sciocco! Sciocco!

The word pounded in Lazzaro's head as he showered

and dressed, beating in his temples like a pulse as he headed down to breakfast.

Fool! Fool for forgetting who she was—and he *had* forgotten.

Holding her, making love to her, kissing her, tasting her, he'd lost himself, lost his mind... For a few blissful hours he had forgotten about everything—Luca, Antonia, the baby, Malvolio...

Lazzaro's face hardened.

She'd lied to him—she still hadn't told him that Roxanne was her cousin, and as for being a virgin!

Lazzaro snapped his fingers at a waitress, jabbed at his cup for her to refill it.

Well, she might have won this round, but the game wasn't over—a fool he'd be no more.

'Good morning!' His deadpan face didn't even change as she staggered into the dining room—utterly business as usual, he was looking through his schedule and tapping away on his laptop as a very untogether Caitlyn rather shakily poured coffee and picked at a croissant.

'Jeremy will drive you back to Melbourne. I have a few things I want to finalise here and I will get the helicopter back—I also need to see to a few things back at the office...'

'I've rearranged our flights.' Somehow she managed to sound efficient. 'Our plane to Rome now leaves at ten. So we need to be at the airport by eight. Do you want me to meet you at the office?'

Lazzaro shook his head. 'Buy a gift for my sister—then you'll need the rest of the day for yourself, to pack, pay bills, whatever...'

So he *did* acknowledge that she actually had a life? Small comfort, though, when she knew she was being got rid of.

'Jeremy and I will pick you up around six-thirty—we can stop at the hospital on our way to the airport.'

'Fine…'

He watched her fumble with her pastry. He could see the bewilderment in her eyes and it angered him—what the hell did she expect? Breakfast in bed?

'Lazzaro!'

Antonia's vibrant greeting caught them both unawares. Caitlyn was just about to sit herself down in the rather opulent waiting room of the private maternity hospital to catch up on some notes while Luca visited his sister before they headed to the airport. In fact, the only reason Caitlyn hadn't stayed in the car with Lazzaro's chauffeur was the fact that she knew Malvolio was still safely at the hotel, and there would be no chance of banging into him. But—looking radiant, pushing a crib along the carpeted corridor from the nursery towards her room—it turned out Antonia was the one who greeted them.

'It is so good to see you—meet your nephew!'

'Shouldn't you be in bed?' Lazzaro frowned, barely giving the infant a glance.

'I was just fetching Luca from the nursery.'

'Don't the nurses do that?' Lazzaro asked, but Antonia just laughed.

'So, what do you think of your new nephew?'

If it had been anyone, *anyone* else, Caitlyn wouldn't have been able to resist peeking into the crib and staring at the newborn. Only her eyes were on Lazzaro, watching every flicker of his reaction as he stared down—and she could see the grief stamped on his face even though he smiled, could see the bob of his Adam's apple as he swallowed while staring at the baby.

'He's beautiful…' His voice was soft, but raw, his hands bunched into fists as if he was fighting with an instinct to touch him.

He looked so lost and wretched that Caitlyn was fighting with instincts of her own, tempted to wrap her fingers around his closed ones, to support him somehow in this difficult time—only that wasn't in Lazzaro's strange rule book, Caitlyn reminded herself. Discretion was the key—and communication outside the sheets taboo.

'Mum says he's the image of you and Luca when you were born.' Antonia was looking at Lazzaro too, her kind, weary face etched with worry, and Caitlyn's heart went out to her. She was sure this was just as impossible for her too.

'Where's Marianna?' Lazzaro dragged his eyes away from the infant. 'Malvolio said she was at the hospital with you.'

'She is—she's with Mum…come on.'

'She's already here?' Lazzaro didn't even attempt to keep the appalled note out of his voice. 'But how?'

'She flew out as soon as she found out I was in labour. If you'd answered your phone, Lazzaro, you'd have known a few hours sooner too! Marco's with her…'

'Marco?' Lazzaro frowned.

'Her boyfriend.'

'Hardly a boy…' Lazzaro sneered, but Antonia wasn't listening.

'Come and say hi—you too,' she offered Caitlyn. 'There's no need to sit in the waiting room. The more the merrier.'

Caitlyn was about to politely decline, positive her presence would be the last thing Lazzaro would want at this intimate family gathering, but just as she was about to shake her head, before the words could even form on her lips, Lazzaro gave a nod.

'Come!' he clipped, in his usual Spartan way, and then he did the strangest thing.

His hand took her elbow and guided her alongside Antonia. And though it was Lazzaro holding her, somehow Caitlyn was sure it was otherwise—sure for a moment that she was the one holding him up—and though common sense argued loudly, told her he was merely being polite, somehow she knew better.

Lazzaro didn't *do* polite.

Entering Antonia's room, he headed over to his mother, kissing her and ignoring Marco, and talking in rapid Italian as Caitlyn hovered uncomfortably.

'Thank you for the flowers.' Antonia smiled at Caitlyn as she opened the gift. 'And thank you for these...' She grinned at Caitlyn's slightly non-plussed look. 'Lazzaro would never say such thoughtful things...or choose something so heavenly.' She held up the tiny outfits Caitlyn had so carefully chosen earlier that afternoon, and the silver rattle that she had hoped was expensive enough to be suitable!

'I *did* put a lot of thought into them!' Lazzaro countered with a half-smile. 'I choose my staff very carefully.'

Although Antonia made an effort to include Caitlyn, Lazzaro's mother ignored her, clearly more than used to having staff around. They spoke in Italian, with Marco bouncing little Marianna on his knee as the *nona* scooped up a sleeping Luca, and though her last week had been spent falling asleep with *Speak Italian in Seven Days* playing in her ears, Caitlyn still really didn't understand a word of the colourful language.

No command of Italian was necessary, though, to comprehend what Lazzaro's mother was saying when she held out the tiny infant and offered him to her son. *'Desiderate tenere il bambino?'*

'Non posso.' Lazzaro shook his head. 'I can't. We have to be at the airport…'

'Surely you can give him a quick cuddle?' Antonia pushed, and though she was smiling, Caitlyn could see tears brimming in her eyes as Lazzaro remained adamant.

'We have to go—there is fog in Europe, and the planes are all off schedule. We really ought to make a move.'

'Do you like my baby brother?' Marianna's eyes, as black as Lazzaro's but a lot more trusting, caught Caitlyn's.

'He's beautiful.' Caitlyn smiled. 'Like his big sister!'

'He's named after my dead uncle.'

And no icy European winter could match the sudden drop in temperature on the hot maternity ward.

'Come.' It was Lazzaro who broke the appalling silence, but his single word unleashed the dam. His mother sped after him, talking in rapid Italian, and as the baby started crying to be fed, unsettled by her new brother, and her uncle who was leaving, so too did Marianna.

So too did Antonia. And her throaty pleas for her brother to just give his mother what she wanted—five minutes of his time—were the ones that finally stalled Lazzaro. A terse nod and a surly shrug implied that there really wasn't an issue, that of course he had no problem spending time with them. Then another brief nod as his mother spoke again.

'We will go for a coffee.' Lazzaro gave his sister a smile 'You feed the baby, we'll take Marianna, then I'll come back and say goodbye.' He glanced over to Caitlyn. 'Meet me in the car in half an hour.'

Which was normal—in the little while she'd been working for him, waiting in reception areas or in the car, chatting to his driver, was a rather regular occurrence, while Lazzaro wined and dined his way through business lunches. Her peripheral presence was necessary in case he wanted her to pluck some figure from her laptop, or—and she still couldn't quite get her head around it—to buy him some mints!

What wasn't normal, though, was being left alone with his sister. What was horribly awkward was pretending nothing untoward had taken place and offering her a smile and rather forced congratulations as she turned to leave. But Antonia's strangled sob as Caitlyn reached the door was utterly heartbreaking, and whether she was Lazzaro's PA or not, whether she was nothing more than a convenience, she was still a woman, and few women could have ignored another in such obvious distress.

'I'm sorry…' Antonia sobbed as Caitlyn came over, her tears spilling onto the screaming baby, his mother's distress making him wail all the louder. 'I'm upsetting Luca…'

'Here…!'

Peeling tissues out of the box on the bedside table, she handed them to the upset woman. When it was clear more than paper was required, Caitlyn relieved Antonia of the screaming baby, rocking him in her arms, trying to hush him as Antonia sobbed on.

'It's all just falling apart…' Antonia was inconsolable.

'I thought with a new baby, if we were all together, then maybe we could move on…' The tears were stilling now, but her distress was just as raw. 'It's never going to get better, is it?'

'Of course it will,' Caitlyn offered helplessly. 'These things take time.'

'It's been more than two years!' Antonia choked. 'Two years of grieving for one brother and watching the other disappear. There was a row, a terrible row, before Luca died. Lazzaro confronted him. Luca was in debt to the eyeballs, spending money like water, completely out of control…'

'I know…' Caitlyn nodded—because she did know, and not just from Roxanne. Like everyone else, she had read the newspapers at the time, watched the journalists deliver the court's findings on the evening news. 'But Lazzaro couldn't have known what was to come…' And he couldn't have, Caitlyn reasoned. He couldn't have known Luca would walk out of the argument and into a bar—would get behind the wheel so loaded that the second he turned the key in the ignition the outcome was inevitable.

'It was Lazzaro's fault.' Antonia's sobbed the words out. 'Why? *Why* would he do that?' Antonia stopped as quickly as she had started, pleading eyes looking to Caitlyn's.

'You said yourself, he *had* to…' Caitlyn attempted. But as Antonia placed her shaking hand over her mouth, closed her eyes in horror, she knew Antonia had said more than she had intended—knew that what she had just heard was something she shouldn't have. 'What happened, Antonia?'

'I can't say…'

She was a pitiful sight. A woman who seemingly had everything—money, looks, a doting husband, beautiful children—only Caitlyn's heart went out to her. Whether Antonia knew it or not, her world really was falling apart. 'I am scared for my brother—scared he is heading down the same path as Luca.'

'Lazzaro doesn't gamble,' Caitlyn soothed, 'and he hardly drinks. Lazzaro—'

'Is in hell…' Antonia finished. 'Just look out for him… You are working with him, closer to him at the moment than his own family.' Antonia's eyes met hers as Caitlyn handed her back little Luca. 'I'm just asking that you look out for him.'

'I somehow don't think Lazzaro would appreciate it.' Caitlyn gave a wobbly smile. The lines were suddenly blurring. He was her boss, nothing else. It was something she had to remind herself of constantly—to remain professional and aloof at all times, and even when he kissed her to somehow remember a kiss was all it was—that even if he had held her last night he had dismissed her in the morning.

Could she do it? Caitlyn wondered as she farewelled Antonia and walked along the hospital corridor. Could she really put her life on hold for him? Fall more and more in love with him? Only to walk away at the end? Because somehow, even when he was loathsome, the more she saw of him, the more she wanted him, and the more he allowed her to have the more she gratefully received—but then what?

What happened when she upped her demands? Would she be dismissed, like Jenna? It was Caitlyn now suddenly near to tears.

When he'd decided he'd had enough, when she'd served her purpose or dared to make a demand, it would be over—

not just a fantasy figure to get over, but her first love to recover from.

'What are *you* doing here?'

Malvolio's voice made her jump, and her eyes darted along the corridor, her heart thudding in her chest as for the first time since he'd tried to kiss her she faced him.

'Lazzaro came to see his sister.'

'I'm not asking about Lazzaro…' Malvolio hissed. 'Stay the hell away from my family—got it?'

Head down, she nodded, walked quickly away. But Malvolio hadn't yet finished.

'Oh, and, Caitlyn—you might think you're on to a good thing, in your fancy new clothes and with your fancy new title, but let me tell you one thing about my brother in-law.' She kept walking, refusing to look back, but his black voice caught up with her before she'd turned the corner. 'He doesn't give a damn about anyone—not even his own family. When he's finished with you—when you've served your purpose—he'll spit you out along with the pips.'

Lazzaro's face was as grim as Caitlyn's when he finally joined her in the car. Climbing in, he didn't even bother to say hello—just told Jeremy to step on it.

'Everything okay?' Finally he deigned to look at her.

'Great!' Caitlyn's eyes met his in the darkness, glittering with tears and holding his for an impossibly long time. 'How about you?'

'Great!' Lazzaro snapped. 'Things couldn't be better.'

CHAPTER SEVEN

THEY breezed through check-in and Customs and took off on time. The journey was in fact perfect—except for the two coiled springs sharing the first-class cabin.

As they hurtled across time zones, Caitlyn played a game with the night sky—convincing herself that the day that had started so perfectly was being extended so it could end on a better note, that somehow he'd look over and smile, as if pleased the universe was giving him these extra hours. Only Lazzaro didn't use them wisely. Barely a word passed between them even as they landed and renegotiated Customs—and stepped out into the freezing morning.

Freezing!

Melbourne winters weren't exactly warm, but they were positively tropical compared to this. Her breath was blowing out white clouds, her teeth chattering as they headed to the waiting car, jumping like a puppy left behind into the heated warmth as the driver loaded their cases.

But nothing—not Lazzaro's black mood nor her earlier confrontation with Malvolio—could dim the beauty of Rome, as the sleek black Mercedes drove them at break-neck speed through the ancient city. She longed to ask the driver to slow down—had to stifle a squeal as the Colosseum came into view.

'It really is in Rome…' She rolled her eyes at Lazzaro's old-fashioned look. 'Right in the middle.' Pressing her nose against the window, at that moment Caitlyn didn't care about his bloody mood, or *her* bloody mood, or what was happening, or where things were going. She was in Rome—*in Rome*—and it was beautiful. The people were beautiful. Stunning groomed women, trailing scarves clipping through the cobbled streets. Elegant men, in long coats… Not caring what Lazzaro thought, she opened the window, closed her eyes for a second against the icy blast of air that hit her, then opened them on a carnival of noise. Mopeds weaving through the heavy traffic, drivers shouting and cursing—she'd never seen so many people. Rush hour in Melbourne was like a Sunday stroll in the park compared to this.

'Close the window,' Lazzaro snapped. 'It's cold.'

'It is!' Pushing the button, blocking out the noise, just for a second, one very defiant second, she looked at him and gave him a little piece of her mind. 'In fact it's probably warmer outside!'

There were five-star hotels, Caitlyn realised as the car door was opened and she stepped out, and then there were *five-star hotels*. Heavy gold revolving doors spun her into a stunning foyer, and Caitlyn didn't know whether to look up or down. Marble pillars stretched to a magnificent high-domed ceiling, and a chandelier surely the size of Caitlyn's back garden, and thick exquisite rugs dotted the black and white tiled floor. And the beauty of her surroundings was only surpassed by the stunning guests.

Ranaldi's Roma was clearly the jewel in the Ranaldi crown.

Lazzaro's bloody mood wasn't aimed solely at her though. After the briefest shower and change in history, with barely a second to take in her stunning suite, there was a sharp rap at her door and work began. Lazzaro met with his staff throughout the day and picked fault with everything—from the food and the selection in the private wine cellar to some unfortunate bellboy whose shirt wasn't tucked in properly. He waltzed through the place, knowing he owned it, and everyone quailed—and Caitlyn trailed. In fact, by the time the old-fashioned lift creaked her up towards her room that evening, not for the first time since taking the position of Lazzaro's assistant, all she felt was exhausted...and not just physically.

His rejection, his cruel dismissal, had cut her to the very core of her being—yet there had been no chance to examine it, no time to process it, to retreat and lick her wounds.

Till now—only now she was too damned tired.

There were no fancy swipe cards here. Instead she opened her door with a key that was as old as time, and thankfully closed the door on the longest day of her life. Her tired eyes took in her suite: the vibrant clash of golds and reds that worked so brilliantly, the intricate flower arrangements, the white shutters at the endless thin windows. Even the vast carved walnut bed couldn't dominate the massive bedroom, but it was the only thing that held her interest. Not even bothering to take off her make-up, Caitlyn dropped her clothes to the floor and brushed her teeth, then sank into bed, trying to summon the energy to book a wake-up call.

She sighed at the soft knocking at her door, choosing to ignore it. She was just closing her eyes as the maid let herself in—no doubt to turn down the bed she was already in…

'Caitlyn…' Though softly spoken, Lazzaro's word made her jump.

'What the hell are you doing in here?' Sitting bolt-upright, she pulled the sheet tightly around her, scarcely able to believe his audacity. 'Don't tell me—you've got a master key to the place.'

'You didn't lock your door,' Lazzaro pointed out, sitting down in the darkness on the bed beside her. 'Look—'

'No!' Without waiting to hear what he wanted, she shook her head. 'I know it's only seven o'clock, I know you warned me that we'd be busy, and you've probably got a million things you want to do this evening and a million people you want to see—'

'Just one.'

'Please,' Caitlyn said, not even attempting to keep the note of weariness out of her voice, 'can't you manage it without me—just this once?'

'Probably,' Lazzaro said, his fingers moving to sheet, his breath warm on her cheek. Caitlyn realised he wasn't here about work. 'Only it wouldn't be anywhere near as nice!'

His depraved response eked out of her the tiniest shocked laugh, and Lazzaro pounced, his mouth claiming hers. But Caitlyn pulled back.

'Don't!' she sobbed. 'You've been vile all day…'

'That was work…' He was raining kisses on her face, his hands pulling her rigid arms to her sides, and, brimming with loathing and longing, she fought to resist as he clouded her mind.

'Not just at work…' He was kissing her quiet, his mouth dulling her words, but again she pulled back. 'You ignored me…'

'I'm not ignoring you now…' Lazzaro husked, then groaned into her neck. 'Caitlyn, please. This endless day has been hell…'

Naked beneath the sheet, her body begged for no more questions. He was here, he'd come to her, somehow he needed her tonight, and it must be enough to hush her worried mind. His hands were cupping her face as he kissed away her doubts, and her sob of anger was aimed at herself as she pulled at his suit, as her fingers tore at his clothes.

Could she do it? Caitlyn begged of herself as he entered her.

Could she be the woman he came to at night if he gave nothing of himself in the morning?

'Yes!' Caitlyn sobbed her answer out loud, then sobbed it again. 'Yes…' she whimpered, her nails digging into the taut muscles of his back as he moved deep within her, tears spilling out of her eyes as he took her to the edge, then toppled her over.

Staring down at her as she slept, her face as pale as the pillow in the moonlight, her hair spread on the sheet, her lips swollen from his attention, her shoulders bruised from his kisses, he knew he was as weak as he was hard.

He had sworn he wouldn't go back—yet here he was. *Sciocco*.

No! Lazzaro's jaw tightened—he was still in control, was wise to her games, was one step ahead. He would trip her up on her lies some time soon…but for now… Pulling her, soft and warm, into his body, he felt her hair tickling his chest as his arm wrapped around her. He stared at the ceiling as the word taunted him again.

Sciocco.

Perhaps a little, Lazzaro conceded, but he could handle it—wouldn't let himself forget for a moment that he was living in a fool's paradise.

'To be the best…' Lazzaro gave her a black smile as they sat in his room on Saturday and for the second time he sent back his food with complaints to the chef '…you have to give the best—every time.'

'Well, my lunch is perfect,' Caitlyn said defiantly—because it was!

She'd been taking notes since eight a.m., a pounding headache her companion as Lazzaro bombarded her with his findings, snapping his fingers as he had the night they'd first met as—not quickly enough for his impatient liking—she retrieved reams and reams of figures from her laptop. She had been grateful, so grateful, when lunch had appeared—and, unlike at the peninsular resort, in-room dining at Ranaldi's Roma was a slice of heaven. A trolley as vast as her dinner table at home had been wheeled in, groaning under the weight of a sumptuous spread of cold meats and pastries, syruped fruits and cannolis, and coffee as thick as treacle had cleared her thumping head—yet still he found something to complain about.

Taking a bite of her cannoli, tasting the sugared creamed cheese, ignoring the inevitable icing sugar moustache, Caitlyn was insistent. 'It's heavenly, in fact.'

'Because *you* know no better!'

God, he was poisonous at times. The man she shared her bed with, shared herself with at night, was unrecognisable against the man she barely tolerated by day.

'Tonight we check out the competition.'

'I thought it was Signor Mancini's party tonight.'

'It is—he is still the competition, and I am his. I can guarantee everything will be perfect—as it should be here. You need to get ready for tonight—your hair is…' He gave her a curious look that inflamed her.

'I didn't wash it this morning,' Caitlyn hissed, 'because I'm having it put up for the party! You-don't-wash-your-hair-the-day-you-get-it-put-up-or-it-comes-down!'

'Thank you for telling me.' He gave her a very on-off smile. 'I was just going to say that you will stand out tonight—there are not many natural blondes in Rome.'

'Oh!' She was jolly well sure he *hadn't* been about to say that, but, given she'd so spectacularly jumped the gun, she'd never know. 'I've chosen one from the dresses you had sent over—don't worry, I won't let you down. So, what are we doing for the rest of the day?'

'I've told you—you are getting your hair and make-up done.'

'It's one p.m.,' Caitlyn pointed out. 'I don't take six hours to get ready!'

He frowned over at her. 'Your eyebrows need doing too…'

'Excuse me?' Caitlyn blushed in anger at yet another rude observation. 'How rude!'

'Tonight you are going to be mingling with Rome's most rich, most beautiful. So I suggest you go and start to prepare. I am just letting you know—'

'Well, don't!' Caitlyn snapped. Her heavenly lunch was

sitting like lead in her stomach, and not for the first time she wondered if she was up to this—wondered if her mother's mortgage was really worth the humiliation. She consoled herself that at least the rose-coloured glasses she'd worn over the years were well and truly starting to clear. 'And if we're being personal…' She stared over at him, wishing he wasn't so damn perfect, trying to find a fault to pick. When there wasn't, annoyed at herself for being so childish, she made one up. 'You've got something on your teeth!'

'I have not.'

'You have,' Caitlyn insisted. 'A great big green bit—right there.' She tapped at her own teeth. 'I just don't want you to embarrass yourself when you abuse your staff!'

He laughed—actually threw his head back and laughed—and, most annoyingly of all, he didn't make a single move to check. Which was probably just as well, Caitlyn thought. Because there was nothing there. Despite herself, she started to laugh too.

'Gone?' He smiled that lazy smile that did something to her deep inside—that made her relent when she'd sworn she wouldn't.

'Gone!' Caitlyn conceded, because for the moment at least it had. Not the imaginary thing on his teeth—they both knew that—but the black cloud that had engulfed them since he'd stepped out of her bed. She was dazzled momentarily by the rainbow of his smile.

'Go!' He said it nicely—rather too nicely, in fact…sort of undressing her with his eyes as he did so…sort of warning her to get out while the going was good. 'Enjoy your afternoon…'

If only she'd picked up her bag then and headed to her suite. But when Lazzaro was being nice there was no one nicer…when Lazzaro was looking at her like that there was every reason to stay.

'Lazzaro…'

The deep, throaty, *familiar* voice made her start. Utterly unprepared, all she could do was sit as he stood, as he took the stunning woman in his arms and kissed her as only Italians did—only there was a tenderness there, a protectiveness there that she'd never witnessed before—and certainly not for herself. There was a gentleness in Lazzaro as he greeted this woman that made Caitlyn's heart bleed.

'Bonita, this is my new personal assistant, Caitlyn Bell—Caitlyn this is Bonita Mancini…' He gave Caitlyn a sudden smile. 'Of course—stupid me. You two will have already met.'

'Met?' Caitlyn frowned, and so too did Bonita.

'We've spoken on the *telefono,* yes?'

'That's right.' Caitlyn nodded, then turned to Lazzaro. 'We've never actually met.'

'But surely at your interview for the PR position…?' Lazzaro was still smiling, but there was a dangerous glint in his eyes. 'Oh—sorry, Caitlyn. I didn't introduce you properly—you see, not only is Bonita Alberto Mancini's wife, she's head of PR. That's how they met, in fact!'

'Still he keeps me working!' Bonita laughed, but her laughter faded as her eyes—not her Botoxed forehead—crinkled in concentration. 'You say you had an interview…?' she attempted, her voice fading as she attempted to place Caitlyn.

'It must have been with another hotel chain.' It was

Lazzaro who broke the appalling silence. 'My mistake.' He might have broken the silence, but nothing could take away the awkwardness—everyone present knew he never made mistakes—at least not when it came to work!

'I'd better get on!' Caitlyn forced a smile and excused herself, reeling from the news that Bonita was Bonita *Mancini,* and looking back just once, in time to see his arm slide around her shoulders and pull her in—in time to see her rest her head on his chest as if she'd missed him for ever.

CHAPTER EIGHT

SHE looked... Caitlyn stared back at her reflection and actually said the word out loud. *'Fabulous!'*

And it had nothing to do with the flattering mirror!

There was no place for self-deprecation tonight—it was about self-preservation. And, oh, the gods had been kind tonight, because if ever she'd needed to pull out all the stops to face Lazzaro, if ever she'd needed to know not just that she was okay, but to *know* she was fabulous—it was tonight.

The hairdressers had practically fallen over themselves to do her hair—and though she'd planned to wear her hair up, in her usual safe French roll, after a glass of champagne and a large boost to her ego Caitlyn had, for the first time in her life, actually listened to what the hairdresser had to say. Instead of staying safe, why not play up her natural asset? Why not wear a head full of blonde curls?

So now she stood, curls snaking around her face and onto her shoulders—her eyes unrecognisable after the skilled attention of the makeup artist.

'Uno o l'altro,' the beautician had explained as she'd scrutinised her face, and Caitlyn had understood—she could play up either her eyes or her mouth, but not both.

The eyes had it!

Slate-grey eyeshadow and lashings of eyeliner and mascara brought out every last glimmer of blue in her eyes, soft blush accentuated her cheekbones, and her lips were full but teasingly neutral. As for the dress—black had never been less safe. A million hand-sewn black glass beads covered every inch of fabric, and the deep empress line showed off her bosom—and from the second she'd slipped it on, feeling guilty for being greedy, Caitlyn had been wanting to ask if it was hers or on loan.

Well, for tonight at least it was hers.

And for tonight at least she had enough confidence to deal with Lazzaro—was enough of a woman to walk away from the man of her dreams.

She'd always thought that he'd come back.

That the bitter man, so twisted by grief, would one day return to the man she had first met. She had been sure in her heart that the man she had fallen in love with was in there somewhere.

Only he wasn't.

Tears glittered in her eyes as the door to her heart closed to him—closed to a man who could do such a thing to his friend. It was all she'd thought about all day, as she was primped and preened to within an inch of her life, to make her fit to grace the arm of Lazzaro Ranaldi when he attended his good friend's birthday party. The friend whose wife he was having an affair with.

'Are you ready?'

It was hardly an effusive greeting, but Caitlyn was relieved not to have to make small talk as she tried to squeeze lipstick, face powder and her key into the tiniest of bags—relieved because in all her efforts to look the part she'd forgotten to prepare herself for the sight of him. Always effortlessly stunning, tonight, when he *had* made an effort, he quite simply took her breath away. Black hair was smoothed back from his face, and his tuxedo was so superbly cut it accentuated his already broad shoulders. The white of his shirt and immaculate trousers highlighted the smooth planes of his stomach and the thick muscular legs that seemed to go on for ever.

'Is that all you're taking?' Lazzaro frowned. 'You know we'll be staying there?'

'Where?'

'At the Mancini hotel—of course.'

She hadn't known, *of course*—though now she thought about it, it seemed obvious. Someone with the wealth and resources of Alberto Mancini would ensure his guests were extremely well looked after.

'It would be rude to decline…' Lazzaro gave a pompous shrug as Caitlyn turned to race to pack an overnight bag. 'Even if my hotel is better.'

'How was your afternoon?' Caitlyn asked as the elevator doors clanged behind them.

'Long,' came the single-word reply as he stared fixedly ahead.

Lazzaro was holding his breath—trying to block out her heady scent—trying not to look at her. Oh, he'd always known she was stunning—that with the right clothes, the right make-up, she could rival any of the A-list beauties who would be paraded tonight—but knowing what he knew, what he'd found out today, seeing her so sleek, so polished, instead of melting him it did the opposite. Tonight she turned him to stone.

He strode out of the lift and across the foyer and into the waiting car. Caitlyn struggled to keep up, tossing her bag to his driver and not offering a single word as the car sped through the wet Rome streets.

A blonde Medusa—bewitching, beguiling. Well, not tonight. Tonight he was impervious to her charms. Tonight he would hold onto the truth—the truth that was becoming clear, no matter how she, how *he,* tried to gloss over it. So many times he'd been tempted to trust her, to ignore the red flags—to just deny what he knew—see only the good… She bewitched him, just as Roxanne had Luca—one look at those eyes and he was gone.

Well, no more!

Tonight he would confront her.

'Lazzaro!'

Alberto Mancini was, of course, the guest of honour at his own party, but Lazzaro clearly came a close second. Their host quickly excused himself from the gathered crowd and made his way over, talking in rapid Italian as he greeted his friend, but politely switching to English as soon as Caitlyn was introduced.

'So, you are Lazzaro's new personal assistant—congratulations! No doubt we will be seeing quite a bit of each other.'

'It's a pleasure to meet you,' Caitlyn dutifully answered.

'May I say you look stunning? Every head turned when you walked in.'

In Lazzaro's direction, Caitlyn wanted to point out. But instead she murmured her thanks.

'This is my wife, Bonita…' Alberto said cheerfully, sliding an arm around his wife's tiny waist as she came over. 'Looking stunning too—though so you should, darling,' he teased good-naturedly, 'with the amount of time you spent at the parlour today! Bonita, this is Caitlyn—Lazzaro's new personal assistant!' And from the tiny nervous dart in Bonita's eye, from her polite response and the kiss on Caitlyn's cheek, if any confirmation had been needed that Alberto knew nothing of his wife's whereabouts that afternoon, then she had it.

As Alberto excused himself and wandered off to mingle with his guests, all pretence at politeness was dropped. Bonita reverted to Italian, taking Lazzaro by the arm and guiding him away, leaving Caitlyn awkward and alone and trying not to show it. She sipped on her drink and made occasional small talk, standing on heels that hurt with a smile that ached—and a heart that was literally breaking.

In a room of beautiful people, somehow Lazzaro topped them all.

He stood just that bit taller, that bit straighter than the rest—with beautiful women floating around him like humming birds, like butterflies…like angry bees, Caitlyn thought sometimes, watching through narrowed eyes as he danced with many—or merely stood as they fought for the beam of his smile, for a second dance with the master, for the chance of a night with him. Alberto Mancini joined him, chatting and laughing and utterly, utterly oblivious—and it made Caitlyn feel sick.

'He's an attractive man…' Bonita was beside her as the painful night was thankfully drawing to a close, sipping on champagne and watching the proceedings. 'Your boss.'

'So is your husband,' Caitlyn answered tightly, her back straightening as if it had a rod in it, her hand so tight on her glass she half expected the stem to snap.

'He is…'

The affection in Bonita's voice confused Caitlyn.

'A lot of people, my family included, think it can only be about money…why would I look at him otherwise? They do not know how he makes me feel.'

'How *does* he make you feel?'

'Safe,' Bonita answered. 'When I am with Alberto, my world is safe.'

Then what the hell are you doing? Caitlyn wanted to scream at her. Only she didn't—just stiffened more, if that were possible, as Lazzaro caught her eye. Her whole body was torn between want and loathing as he excused himself from the masses and made his way over.

'We were just talking about you, Lazzaro.' Bonita smiled.

'All good, I hope?' he drawled, but his face was grim. 'I think Alberto has had enough.'

'I agree.' Bonita gave a tight smile. 'Will you…?'

'I have told him.' Lazzaro nodded. 'He is just saying his farewells—I will help him to his room.' His eyes were thoughtful as he looked over at Caitlyn. 'I'm sorry if I have left you to your own devices…'

'I'm not your date, Lazzaro,' Caitlyn answered tightly. 'This is work.'

'Then, when I return, it's time I asked my assistant to dance.'

A heart that should be utterly unmoved by him somehow leapt when finally they danced.

Even as he held her, even as they danced, it was at arm's length—the boss and his assistant—the duty dance. But even if his hands barely touched her dress, even if her body wasn't against his, the energy was undeniable—the space between them thick with loathing and bitter attraction. Her hair occasionally tickled his cheek, her scent filled his nostrils, and the awkwardness between them was arousing somehow. He wanted to bury his face in her hair, to pull her soft, warm body to his hard one, but instead he spoke.

'Thank you…' His voice was low in her ear. 'For not saying anything to Alberto about this afternoon.'

'Don't thank me.' His hands were loosely around her waist, their bodies somehow close enough to look as if they were comfortable with each other even while barely touching—oh, but she ached, longed to move that danger-ous couple of inches, to rest herself against him, to close her eyes and feel him, have him hold her. But Caitlyn knew if she did she'd be lost. 'Don't make me a part of it.'

'I'm not with you—a part of it?' Now and then he did that—his English was seemingly not quite so perfect, needing her to translate—but Caitlyn knew better. Knew he was, in fact, just buying a little more time.

'Don't…' She looked up to him. 'Don't ever put me in that position again. I'll lie to your girlfriends, Lazzaro—but not to their partners.'

'I never asked you to lie…'

'Should I have told him Bonita and I had already met?' Her words hissed into his ears. 'When she came to your suite. Should I have told him that the reason his young gold-digging wife's looking so fabulous—with that flush on her face and her sparkling eyes—has nothing to do with hours at the salon, but everything to do with your—?' Her voice stopped abruptly as his hand caught her wrist.

His words were caustic as they reached her. 'How dare you judge me by your own standards?'

'At least I *have* some standards!'

They weren't even pretending to dance now, just standing in the middle of the dance floor, bristling, bursting with unsaid words. But thankfully the music paused then, the room rippling with applause, and Lazzaro's hand tightened around hers, practically dragging her across the dance floor to a secluded table.

Only there was no such thing as total seclusion when you were Lazzaro Ranaldi. A waiter appeared—offering drinks, pouring water—when all they wanted was to be left alone.

'What standards?' Lazzaro sneered, picking up the conversation exactly where they had left it. *'You're* the liar...'

'Me?'

'It was confirmed today—you never did have a second interview lined up with Mancini.' He watched as she coloured up, watched her hands tighten around her drink, and couldn't help but smile in triumph. It was Caitlyn playing for time now. 'You never even had a *first!'*

'No,' Caitlyn finally answered, glad for the water that had been poured—glad that there was actually something she could do with her hands as she fiddled with her glass.

'You never even sent them your résumé, did you?'

'Why bother asking when clearly you've been checking up?'

'Of course,' Lazzaro answered evenly. 'What? Did you think that I wouldn't? Did you expect me to just trust you? Did you think that I really thought I had the hotel name wrong?'

'I'm surprised you had time to even think of me when you were with Bonita,' Caitlyn spat. 'I'm surprised I even entered you head.'

'I don't have to explain myself to you.' In a curiously insolent gesture Lazzaro raised one shoulder, then dropped it. 'But clearly, after your little display, it has slipped your mind that I am in fact your boss, and you *do* have to explain yourself to *me!* So, why did you lie?'

But suddenly he changed his mind—the question he had just voiced temporarily forgotten as angrily he leant over the table.

'Alberto Mancini is my friend—how dare you insult me—*how dare you insult Bonita too*—when you know nothing of what has gone on? Nothing!'

'Then tell me,' Caitlyn begged. 'What the hell am I supposed to think, Lazzaro? She's on the phone every five minutes, and coming up to your room, and clearly Alberto doesn't have a clue…'

'Why would I tell you? I don't trust you,' Lazzaro sneered. 'So come on—why did you lie?'

'I just did.' Caitlyn shrugged tightly.

'Surely in an interview you must—'

'When I *lied,*' Caitlyn interrupted, 'I wasn't even aware I was *being* interviewed. In fact, if I remember correctly, when I *lied* to you, Lazzaro, I was trying to *leave* my job, not wangle another one.'

'You said you had another job practically lined up,' Lazzaro pointed out. 'You specifically said—'

Caitlyn put down her drink and stood up—she didn't

need this sort of inquisition now, didn't want to go over that awful day again. And she was also angry—angry at the accusing way he always looked at her, the accusing way he so *often* looked at her.

'Oh, I lied,' Caitlyn flared, 'and you were bloody grateful at the time, if I remember rightly. Grateful that you didn't have to explain to your precious sister the type of man she was married to—grateful that you could put another Band-Aid over a raw subject rather than deal with it!'

'I never asked for you to lie! I told you I wanted the truth.'

'Perhaps!' People were looking at them now, heads turning in their direction—the Italians were not exactly known for their discretion—but Caitlyn couldn't have cared less. 'But please don't sit there and try to tell me you weren't just a little bit relieved when you didn't have to face up to it, didn't have to actually deal with it—just like you don't want to deal with your br—' Her mouth snapped closed, her voice abruptly halting as if a plug had suddenly been pulled.

'Go on.' His voice was like ice. 'Finish what you were going to say.'

'I—I don't want to…' Caitlyn stammered, horrified at what she had just said, horrified at where this argument had led. But Lazzaro wasn't letting her leave it there.

'What is it I don't want to deal with?'

'Lazzaro, don't.'

'Clearly you have an opinion on me,' Lazzaro continued, utterly ignoring her words. 'And I'd like to hear it!'

There was no chance of even pretending this evening was going to conclude politely—no chance of making small talk when the big talk was hanging in the air. 'I should go…'

She stood up. Hand shaking, Caitlyn reached for her bag—but Lazzaro caught her wrist. 'Why would you leave when the conversation is just starting to get interesting?'

'I'm going to bed.' She pulled back her hand, and he let her go, but even as she turned, even as her shaking legs tried to walk her out of the ballroom, she knew that he was behind her.

Momentarily she lost direction—the Mancini lobby was unfamiliar—but, locating the lifts, she clipped towards them, knowing it wasn't over. Without looking over her shoulder, Caitlyn closed her eyes as he stepped in the lift beside her, but her eyelids couldn't dim the burn of his eyes on her. Her body was drenched in his anger—her mind trapped in the maze of a row that hadn't yet happened but, thanks to her careless words, it would seem now had to.

He walked her to her door uninvited, leant against the wall without a word as it took her three goes to get the blasted swipe card to work, and even as she stepped in, even as she went to close the door, she knew she hadn't seen the last of him.

'What?' His face twisted into a smile that was completely false as his foot jammed the door. 'Aren't you even going to ask me in for coffee?'

And she nodded—because it wasn't him she feared, but what she had unleashed in the terrible, public moment she'd so poorly chosen to discuss his private agony. Or maybe it had been the right moment, Caitlyn reflected as she stepped back enough to let him in. Because he hadn't silenced her, or halted her…hadn't run from the issue—in fact, he'd followed her here to face it.

The room had been prepared—the bed turned back, chocolates placed on her pillows—and she stood there trembling.

'You were saying?'

'Your brother.' Finally she concluded what she had to say—the plug back in, the power back on. And the light was a relief after the darkness they had plunged into. It had been a necessary darkness, though, Caitlyn realised—the panic, the fumbling, the searching, all needed to bring them to this point, where finally she could look at him as she said the word that no one was really allowed to. 'Luca.'

'I deal with Luca's death every day.' Lazzaro attempted a dismissal.

'Every minute of every hour of every day,' Caitlyn countered, watching as he closed his eyes. 'I know you must feel awful…'

'You know, do you?'

'My grandfather died six months ago—'

'You compare the death of a young man—'

'No!' Caitlyn interrupted with a shout of her own. 'No, but I know how it feels to miss someone, and I know how it feels to love and mourn someone. But I also know peace, Lazzaro, something that seems to elude *you* even two years on!' Her voice was softer now. 'I know you rowed before he died—I read it in the papers, and Antonia said it was awful. But by all accounts Luca was out of control, something had to be said—and I don't get it. You'd have been prepared for his anger. How did you let him hit you? How—?'

'Drop it!' His voice had a stern warning ring—angry, even. Only it wasn't aimed at her, instead it was turned onto himself. The past few days had been hell—the past few weeks, in fact. Knowing his family would soon all be together, that Luca's name would be said again. Like living in a sewer—the filth and grime seeping through the floorboards no matter how much he tried to gloss it over. And now here she stood—understanding in her voice, eyes that seemed to reach inside him—and it would be so, so easy to push aside doubt, to convince himself that she actually was different, that here was someone he could tell.

And how he wanted to tell. Only Malvolio's warning was ringing in his ears like the doomsday bell, and eyes as blue as Roxanne's eyes were staring back at him, just as they had that fateful day.

'It shouldn't be like that, Lazzaro…'

'How should it be, then?' Lazzaro fixed her with his glare, tried to warn her off—to get her the hell back—tried to ward her off, tried to keep his head, before she melted his heart again.

'I don't know…'

'That's right, you *don't* know—you don't know,' he repeated. 'So don't tell me I'm not dealing with things properly when you have no idea what happened that day.'

'Tell me, then,' Caitlyn begged.

'Why?' he asked.

'Because I want to know.'

'Why?'

'Because…' Like pulling the cork on a champagne bottle, she could feel the trepidation, feel the pressure building inside, and she didn't want to do it, didn't want to release what was inside. Only she couldn't hold it back, and just closed her eyes as she let it out—as the cork hit the wall and words spilled and bubbled and overflowed. 'Because I care about you, Lazzaro—and I'm sorry if that's not what you want to hear, or if it troubles you. I'm sorry if I'm not supposed to have feelings for you and I'm only supposed to be around when my services are required, but I happen to care about you—'

'What?' He was practically sneering. 'You want me to open up to *you*?' He mocked her with a black laugh. 'So you can use it on me later?'

'Why would I use it on you later?'

'You contradict yourself,' Lazzaro jeered, because it was easier—easier to keep her at arm's length than let her drag him in. 'One minute I am the lowest form of life—a man you say would sleep with his friend's wife—yet in the next breath you tell me you care. How?' he roared. 'How could you care about someone like that?'

'I don't know,' Caitlyn whispered. 'I just know that I do.'

There was the longest silence—his eyes were scales that weighed her up, his mind was begging him to see reason. Only he didn't want to.

Really didn't want to.

He wanted her to care—because so did he.

'Caitlyn, I have not slept with Bonita—I would never do that—I'm asking you to believe me.'

'Bonita's not the problem…' Thick black tears were rolling down her cheeks. She knew that because she saw the streaks on her hand when she wiped them away, pathetically grateful when he peeled off a wad of tissues and handed it to her. 'I'm just not up to this, Lazzaro. Hot one minute, cold the next…I don't understand why sometimes you choose to hate me…'

'Look, can we just start again?' His usually steady voice was rapid, interrupting her. 'Can we forget all that has been and start again?'

'Can we?' She truly didn't know.

'I can.' Lazzaro nodded.

'And you won't hate me again in the morning?'

'I never hated you…' Lazzaro said slowly. 'How can I hate you when all I do is want you?'

But it wasn't enough. She knew that, *knew* that, but she couldn't question him, didn't want to question him further, because his mouth was on hers, and it was surely sweeter than the truth.

His mouth was ravaging hers—his want matching hers—and the earth shifted as he moved closer into her space. She could hear the zipper of her dress as he pulled it down, the chill of air on the small of her back, and she braced herself for his hand on her bottom. At that moment she would have forgiven him for heading down instead of up—only he didn't. Each rib, each space was fingered with such lingering expertise that her panties were a damp mass when finally he found her bra, unhooked it. But instead of removing her top, instead of undressing her, he lowered his head and kissed her through her dress and the lace of her bra, his teeth nibbling round each areola, her dry-clean-only dress neither dry nor clean as still he worked on. His greedy hands pulled her dress down at the straps, and a thousand glass beads cascaded to the floor, crushed beneath their feet in the race to get out of their clothes. But there was no time. Caitlyn was whimpering with need to have her hungry nipple in his mouth, and if he hadn't taken it then she'd have begged.

It hurt.

Oh, but it was a delicious hurt as his mouth stretched her nipple to its greedy length. His lips paused, then he smiled up at her and suckled till it was indecent, till Caitlyn was moaning, her hand fumbling with his trousers, with his belt. One need was satisfied and she was greedy for more now, as still he suckled, trying to get rid of things that didn't matter to reach the things that did.

She was naked from the waist up and flaming from the waist down, but still he paid her breasts lavish attention as he slid her panties down her thighs. And the bed was just a little bit too far, so the dressing table sufficed, the mirror cold against her back, the surface hard against her bottom. But absolutely the pain was worth the gain, and the angled mirrors gave her never-ending views of him as she laid her head on his shoulder. She gazed at their reflection, saw his arms tighten around hers as he slid inside her, could see her thighs wrapped around his waist as she pulled him in closer, see the dint in his buttocks as her hands went there.

'Lazzaro…' she pleaded, and she wasn't looking any more, but sucking, biting on his salty shoulder, dragging her lips as she tried to hold it in.

But thankfully he wasn't taking his time tonight. He was swelling deeper inside her as she coiled into him, and she wasn't sure if it was people in the next room knocking or the thud of the mirror against the wall, didn't even care *where* they were as he arched his body and leant back, as somehow he climbed deeper inside her…as somehow he took just a little bit more than she knew she should give.

And after, when they were in bed, when maybe she should have just left it, bravely she didn't. Boldly, yet terribly tentatively, her fingers traced the length of his jagged raised scar. She watched as he closed his eyes—not gently, but sort of squeezing them together, as if anticipating the hurt her touch would cause, as if the wound was still raw—and Caitlyn knew then that it was.

'What happened here?'

His fingers caught hers, closed around them. Caitlyn was sure he was about to pull her hand away, and mentally kicked herself for asking too much too soon, but instead of pushing her away his fingers straightened her hand out, till it was the cool of her palm pressing against his cheek. And though they'd just made love, though never in her life had she felt so close to another human being, for that atom of time they weren't just close, they were together—his pain hers, her comfort his to have.

The tension permanently etched in his features faded away as she leant forward, soft lips on his wound, trying to kiss away the agony. Her salty tears bathed his scar, but only for a little while. Not roughly, but gently, he pushed her away, turned his face away from hers as she voiced the question again.

'What happened that day, Lazzaro?'

But even though she'd asked, even though she was sure she could deal with it, his voice told her that maybe she couldn't. The hollows of his pain and raw grief were so evident it made her wince, made her close her eyes as, albeit gently, and albeit tenderly, this time he pushed her away with three little words.

'Ask your cousin.'

'Going anywhere?' Brave, but scared, she smiled down at him the next morning.

Two strikes and he was out for good was her unwritten rule—but Lazzaro's eyes weren't avoiding hers this morning. In fact, utterly relaxed, he even managed to make her laugh.

'Just to my room…' His hand was under the sheet, exploring her shamelessly. 'I'll meet you at breakfast and tell you what our plans are until our flight this evening.'

'Go, then…' Caitlyn grinned. She loved him all of the time, but liked him more when he was like this.

'You *know* the only place I'm going,' Lazzaro drawled, making her gasp as he did something indecent, 'is here.'

'How was your night?' Alberto Mancini beamed over them.

The mood was rather more relaxed as his intimate, though very well-bred friends gathered for a lavish breakfast.

'I trust you were comfortable?'

'The bed was a bit lumpy,' Lazzaro teased good-naturedly. 'But for a second-rate hotel—not bad!'

'Come,' said Alberto. 'I am going to speak with the minister and his lovely wife—and before I make my speech, can I borrow your boss?'

'Of course.' Caitlyn smiled, swallowing hard when Bonita slipped into Lazzaro's vacant seat.

'Thank you,' she said, 'for your discretion yesterday. I am so glad last night is over. If it wasn't for Lazzaro, I don't know how we'd have got through.' She gave a tired smile. 'I know that Lazzaro tells his PA everything.'

'Not this one…' Caitlyn started, but her voice faded as Alberto took the floor, greeting his guests, thanking them for coming. That much Caitlyn understood, but after a moment he handed the microphone to Lazzaro, and she watched as he spoke on his friend's behalf. Whatever he said made everyone laugh—only not Bonita. Her hand was dry as it reached for Caitlyn's.

'Thank God for Lazzaro…' Bonita said in a strangled whisper. 'Alberto is forgetting names, slurring his words sometimes—I did not want him to look a fool, or for people to think he was drunk, so I asked Lazzaro to stick by him…to cover for his memory lapses…' She dabbed at her cheek with a handkerchief, then saw Caitlyn's shocked expression, and for a second it was Bonita consoling Caitlyn.

'You really didn't know? Lazzaro never told you?'

'I thought…' Caitlyn winced in misery, but Bonita actually laughed.

'What *must* you have thought? Oh, but you are new—you would not know what a wonderful man he is just yet.'

Oh, but she was starting to.

'Alberto is sick,' Bonita explained, her voice brave, but her hand slipping into Caitlyn's again, and clinging onto it as she spoke. 'He is to start treatment as soon as possible, but we want to wait—his daughter gets married soon. Just two more weeks is all we are asking,' Bonita rasped. 'If we can just hold it together for two weeks, till his daughter gets married—*then* we can tell everyone.'

Just for a second Caitlyn met Lazzaro's gaze—guilt and regret were washing over her for her harsh assumptions—for thinking the very worst of him. And she was proud too—proud that even last night, with his back to the wall, he hadn't betrayed his friend's trust.

Hadn't told her the truth when it would surely have been so much easier for him.

CHAPTER NINE

'I WISH you'd told me,' Caitlyn said, wondering how the sky could be so blue and the sun could be out, yet it was so cold as they emerged from the hotel. Finally she was to be treated to a real glimpse of the Eternal City...

'It wasn't my place to tell.'

'So you let me think the worst?'

'You chose to think the worst,' Lazzaro pointed out.

'So do you...' It was the hardest thing she'd ever said, offering a fact that was only based on her feeling. 'Lazzaro, surely it's something we should talk about—?'

'Not today.' He silenced her with a kiss. 'Let's just enjoy today.'

There were only a few hours till they headed back to Australia—and though she'd braced herself for coldness, for distance between them, it was anything but. And once breakfast was over, he'd suggested they spend the day wandering Rome.

They stopped in tiny cafés, where Caitlyn practised her appalling Italian and Lazzaro winced in apology at the waiters. She took her camera out at every turn. She ate chestnuts out of the bag, and, even though they were possibly the most disgusting thing she had ever tasted, somehow she finished the lot.

'You should get a memento…' Lazzaro was steering her towards shops with names that were more likely to be represented by fakes in her wardrobe. But even though she'd probably rue it later, even though her friends would never understand, and even though they were the most glamorous she'd ever seen, the boutiques around Piazza di Spagna held little interest for Caitlyn—even when Lazzaro prompted her to choose a bag, 'or shoes, or whatever it is that women like.'

'I like walking.'

So they did—moving away from the shops to the Spanish Steps themselves, where Caitlyn, just a little bit shy, pulled out her camera again and asked Lazzaro to take her photo. Blushing, she shook her head when a cheerful tourist offered to take the camera and take a photo of the two of them.

'Thank you, but no…'

'Why not?' Lazzaro laughed at her blush as they walked on. 'Don't you want to remember us together today?'

She would *always* remember today—with or without a photo—would always remember walking around the most stunning of cities with the most stunning of men. Would always remember the thrill of the feel of his hand slipping into hers. For a little while they were just another couple—another pair of lovers wandering the streets talking about nothing and everything, watching the world go by—and for today at least it was a nicer world with the other there.

She didn't need her tourist guide to know they were at the Trevi Fountain—didn't need to ask what Lazzaro was doing when he rummaged in his pocket and offered her a coin.

'You know the saying…' His hand was absolutely steady as he offered her the coin. 'If you throw in a coin, it is guaranteed you will be back—take it.'

Only she didn't know if she wanted to.

No matter how beautiful the city was, it could never be as beautiful as it was today—and Caitlyn truly didn't know if she wanted to come back if it wasn't with him. She wanted to remember it just as it was.

Oh, today they were fine, between the sheets they were fine—when it was just them, just the two of them and nothing else came close, then there was nothing better—only somehow she knew it couldn't last. Their world was a fragile bubble that somehow couldn't survive the elements.

'Take it.'

And finally she did—watched as it sank to the bottom and joined a million other wishes—closed her eyes as he put his arm around her—leant on him for just a little while longer—tried to convince herself they were really okay—that the little bit they had was enough to sustain them in the real world.…

CHAPTER TEN

THEY *did* have enough to sustain them.

As long as they were careful—as they long as they weren't greedy and lived solely in the moment—didn't look at the past or glimpse the future. As long as he made love to her at night and kissed her in the morning—as long as they didn't address the issues—*then* they were okay.

'Hi, Mum!' Sitting at her desk a week after they returned, Caitlyn couldn't keep the happiness from her voice. But she checked it a touch as the thought of her mother's problems brought her rapidly back down to earth. 'How are things?'

'Great!' Her unusually effusive responsive had Caitlyn frowning.

'Great?' Caitlyn checked.

'The lawyer just called—we've won!' Her voice broke then, laughter turning to tears. 'We can keep the house.'

And even though their lawyer had said over and over that Cheryl had no case, that her grandfather's wishes had been clear, that her mother's contribution to the home had been documented, to have it confirmed, to know that it was finally over brought such a sweet flood of release that only then did Caitlyn actually realise the strain she had been under.

'Thank you…' Helen cried into the phone. 'I know what I've put you through. I know it wasn't fair to ask you to take on such a huge mortgage…'

'I didn't have to, though!' Caitlyn smiled.

'But you would have,' her mother pointed out.

'And you did,' Caitlyn said softly. 'You did it for your dad, remember?'

'Why wouldn't they have a bridal registry?' Lazzaro was utterly perplexed as, smiling, she walked into his office. 'Of all the stupid things… What are *you* looking so happy about?'

'I just am.'

She'd never told him about her problems. The sum of money that was so huge to her was a drop in the ocean to Lazzaro, and worse for Caitlyn than him not understanding would have been the prospect of him sorting it out— the idea of somehow being beholden to him. As she took Alberto Mancini's daughter's wedding invitation from him, her smile widened. 'I actually think it's nice that they don't have a registry! It means that people like you can't just click their mouse and have their gift dispatched—it means pompous, arrogant people like you actually have to stop and think about what their friends might want for a wedding gift.'

'They are not my friends.' Lazzaro flicked his hands skywards in exasperation. 'She is the *daughter* of a *friend* of mine—a daughter I have not seen for five years, and I have never even *met* her fiancé. How could I possibly know what they want?'

'Well, you'd better think fast,' Caitlyn said cheekily. 'You fly out on Thursday.'

'Come with me.'

'I can't.' Caitlyn groaned. 'I know you're used to it, Lazzaro, and I know we'll be travelling first-class and I can sleep all the way there—I know all that—but honestly...'

'Okay—I get it...' he relented. 'You need your weekend off.'

'I do.'

And, oh, she did. Just needed a weekend to catch up with friends, to sleep in, to see her mum, to read... Lazzaro had said the job would be demanding, and it was, but add to the most demanding of jobs the most demanding of lovers, and Caitlyn was actually looking forward to a weekend of...nothing.

'So you're definitely not coming.' He gave a regretful smile, then shot her a look that had her in flames. 'Which means I won't be either.'

'You'll survive!' Caitlyn gave a saucy wink.

'I guess I'll have to—but for your sins *you* can choose the gift.' He waved away her protest. 'That is why us pompous, arrogant people have assistants—off you go.'

What did you get someone who had everything? Someone you'd never met, someone who... Racking her brains, Caitlyn trailed the shops, wishing she knew enough to come back with something fabulous and meaningful... Why the hell *didn't* they have a bridal registry? Caitlyn thought as she trudged back a couple of hours later to the hotel—defeated and empty-handed, but still smiling. She'd splurged on a bottle of champagne—she would bung it in the fridge at work and open it the second she got home tonight...

'Ms Bell?' Caught unawares, Caitlyn started at the sound of her name, swinging around and frowning at the woman who promptly thrust a microphone under her nose. 'What do you have to say about the rumours that Lazzaro Ranaldi is dating his rival's wife?'

'Pardon…?' Like a rabbit in headlights, Caitlyn froze as she saw the television camera zooming in on her.

'We have it from a reliable source that Mr Ranaldi has been seeing rather a lot of Bonita Mancini—we have photos of them at lunch, and we have heard that he spent the afternoon of Mr Mancini's sixtieth birthday with her. And that night he put him to bed drunk and then consoled his wife—'

'No!' Caitlyn's denial was immediate, her mind whirring. It was just a week to the wedding—all Bonita had wanted was for her stepdaughter to marry before hearing the news that her father was terminally ill—and now somehow the press had twisted what few facts they had into something sordid.

'But Mrs Mancini *did* spend the afternoon in Mr Ranaldi's suite…?'

Caitlyn didn't answer. Two spots of colour were burning on her cheeks, and she wished she was better prepared for this. She knew, as Lazzaro's assistant, that she should have just walked away at the outset, should have said nothing, should neither have confirmed or denied.

'And she did spend the night with Mr Ranaldi?'

'No.' Caitlyn was adamant now. 'She didn't.'

'How can you be sure? My sources state that—'

'I'm quite sure Mr Ranaldi didn't spend the night with Mrs Mancini.' She knew even as she said it that she would regret it, but knew she had no choice. She had to quash the rumours now.

'And you're sure because…?'

And even if it was a rushed decision it wasn't blind—Caitlyn could still feel Bonita's hand in hers, feel the love that everyone denied she had for her husband, and she knew that even if it wasn't what was wanted, it was something she had to do.

'I'm sure he wasn't with Mrs Mancini, because Lazzaro Ranaldi spent the night with me.'

Turning, she walked away—away from the hotel—disappearing into the crowds, wondering how she would face him, wondering what Lazzaro's reaction would be when he heard what she'd done…

Never for a second did she imagine the truth.

The frown on his face as he watched after his sister rang him on his mobile and told him to turn on the news, the black anger as he heard the reporter's allegations.

His hand jerked to his desk phone, to ring Bonita and warn her, but his grim face broke into a smile as he heard her blurt out her admission—as Caitlyn Bell dragged them out to face the world.

'She's lovely…' a forgotten Antonia said down his mobile.

'Not exactly discreet, though!' Lazzaro pointed out, but he was still smiling.

'So what are you going to do about it, brother?'

He didn't answer straight away, just stared out of his vast window down to the city streets below, knowing she was down there—imagining her embarrassment, her horror at what she had done, and wanting to soothe it.

To tell her it was okay.

To tell her that *they* were okay.

For the first time in the longest time he breathed

without pain. For just a moment or two Lazzaro felt peace creep somewhere into his soul—glimpsed a future that was bearable.

'Lazzaro?' Antonia pushed excitedly, smiling herself when her brother spoke again, then hung up the phone.

'*We'll* let you know.'

But numbing a toothache didn't make the rot go away. Even if the pain was deadened for a while, still the damage went on inside—weakening the roots, prolonging the inevitable, till it erupted in an agony that couldn't be escaped. And then extraction was preferable to treatment.

As Lazzaro clicked off the phone, as he wondered if he should just ring her now and tell her to stop hiding, the door opened and his smile faded—as the one woman on God's earth he'd hoped never to see again walked into his office and plunged him out of his momentary oasis and straight back into hell.

CHAPTER ELEVEN

'WHAT the hell do *you* want?' Lazzaro sneered out the words, contempt blazing in his eyes as he stared at the person he hated most in the world. 'Who let you in?'

'Audrey let me up—she still remembers me.' Roxanne flicked back her dark curls, strode across his office as if she owned it. ' I thought we should clear the air…'

'Clear the air?' Lazzaro spat. 'The air stinks when you're here. The stench of you makes me—'

'Better out than in!' Roxanne's red lips smiled sweetly at him. 'I saw Caitlyn on the news—she's good, I have to admit that. When she sets her mind on something she always gives it her best.'

'What?' Lazzaro snapped, then shook his head—because he didn't want to hear it, didn't need to hear, didn't want to be in the same room as Roxanne for even a second. 'Get out, Roxanne—you make me sick.'

'Did you fund her lawyers, Lazzaro?'

'Lawyers?' Narrowed eyes watched his smudge of a frown appear. 'I don't know what you're talking about.'

'You mean she didn't tell you? Did sweet little Caitlyn forget to mention when she had her legs wrapped around you that, even though her mother had freeloaded off my grandfather for years, not satisfied with living there, because Helen Bell couldn't afford to raise her bastard child herself, even after he died they refused to move out, that they're refusing to give my mother her fair share?'

'You're full of it,' Lazzaro sneered. 'You couldn't tell the truth on your deathbed.' A thud of papers on his desk held his gaze for a second. Legal letters. He pointedly pushed them away, but he was rattled now—and she knew it.

'Why would I lie?' Roxanne stared at him, those blue eyes the same as Caitlyn's, but utterly, utterly steady—not even a hint of a flicker as they pinned him—and at that moment Lazzaro truly didn't know what was real and what wasn't. Whether it was Roxanne looking him in the eye and lying, or Caitlyn who couldn't.

'Knowing Caitlyn, you were probably her plan B.'

'What do you want, Roxanne?' He gave a mirthless laugh. 'As if I didn't already know.'

'I want what my mother's entitled to.'

'If she's so entitled the courts would have seen it that way.'

'Unlike Caitlyn, I don't have access to limitless funds to pay lawyers—unlike my cousin, I'm not screwing a Ranaldi!' Her face twisted with bitterness. 'You really think she's all sweetness and light, don't you? You're so bloody quick to make out I'm the bitch here.'

'That goes without saying.'

'You know, she always said she'd get you in the end…' Roxanne watched his jaw tighten, but he shook his head.

'You're a liar, Roxanne,' Lazzaro hissed. 'You're just rotten to the core.'

'I can still see her the day before Luca died, with that

stupid photo of you she carried around, rattling on about how you'd given her a lift home and how she was already a shoe-in.' Watching his face pale, watching as a muscle pounded in his cheek, Roxanne was sure that she had him. 'Anyway I'm tired of playing with lawyers. Journalists are far more fun—they actually pay to listen—and I'm sure they'd be delighted to hear the full story about Luca!'

'How much do you want?' Pulling out his chequebook, somehow Lazzaro's hands were steady—but his face was as white and as cold as marble.

'My mother's share.' Roxanne spat out the figure, her blue eyes boring into his as he wrote not the sum she quoted, but two *very* choice little words. He watched her greedy hand snatch the cheque from his, watched her mouth twist in rage as she read his none too polite request for her to leave.

'Talk to your journalist,' Lazzaro jeered as she screwed it up and hurled it at him. 'But, as you pointed out, I have limitless funds—and if you do talk I will spend whatever it takes to ensure you never see a single cent. I tell you now that I will devote the rest of my life to making yours hell. Never threaten me again, Roxanne, and never try to bribe me. I don't deal with dirt!'

'Oh, but you do, Lazzaro—and, just like your brother, you're too foolish to realise!' She turned at the door, excising her jealousy, her venom, her hatred, with every spiteful word. 'The only difference between Caitlyn and me is that she chose more wisely. My cousin happened to hitch her star to the *right* wagon!'

Her smell lingered long after she'd left—a sickly-sweet perfume that seeped into his pores, the same sickly scent she'd had on that day…here, right here. Sinking into his seat, he closed his eyes, waited for the nausea to recede— only it didn't.

'Luca…' He closed his eyes. He could see his brother's face. The face that had always been the same as his was different, and it wasn't just the years of agony, regret and bitterness that had wreaked changes… Lazzaro's fingers ran along the jagged line on his cheekbone—the numb knot of flesh, the scar that Luca had inflicted on his last day on earth.

Still numb.

Memories he'd spent more than two years quashing were bobbing to the surface now, and no matter how quickly he pushed one down, another popped up. He was locked in a shooting range—each image a target, each picture shot down, only to reappear stronger and more relentless than before.

Two years on the pain was still just too big to deal with— but, like an anaesthetic wearing off, sensation was starting to creep in, raw wounds that weren't ready to be exposed yet were starting to make themselves known.

Only he didn't want to feel—didn't want to face it.

But that was exactly what Caitlyn did—she made him face the impossible.

As soon as she walked into his office, Caitlyn realised he couldn't have heard her knock. Knew, somehow, that she was glimpsing a side to Lazzaro Ranaldi that he would prefer no one, not even his lover, to see.

His head was in his hands, his shoulders slumped, his complexion grey beneath his fingers. She should turn, Caitlyn thought, walk out and knock again, save them both the embarrassment of explanations. But in that frozen second he looked up.

'I'm sorry…' She spilled the words out. 'What I said to the press—I know it was indiscreet, I know I should have called you straight after. I was just so embarrassed…'

His expression gave her nothing, no clue at all, and even though he was looking at her it was as if he was looking straight through her—as if he wasn't even hearing her.

'I was just put on the spot. I knew how important it was that it didn't come out about Alberto, what it would do to him if there was even a hint of an affair…'

The clap of his hands was like the crack of a whip, making her jump, making her eyes widen in confusion as it continued—as Lazzaro leant back in his chair and gave a slow hand-clap, on and on, as she stood there mute.

'Bravo, Caitlyn.' He'd stopped clapping now, but still it echoed in her head, stinging her ears as he stared at her now—stared at her as if he hated her. 'You're wasted as a PA. You should try your hand on the stage after I fire you.'

'Because of what I said to the press—?' she started, but her words were cut off by his.

'Don't play a player, Caitlyn. Especially not one as good as me.'

'A player? I don't know what you mean.'

'She's still playing…' Lazzaro jeered to an absent crowd. 'Hey, why the champagne, Caitlyn? Come on—get out the glasses…'

'I don't know what you mean…'

Tears were pricking her eyes, her head spinning, but he pulled two from the shelf and grabbed the bottle, popping the cork against the wall as a sob escaped her lips.

'What are we celebrating?' Lazzaro smiled, but his eyes were black with hatred. 'Your little announcement about us to the press? Or the fact you've screwed your cousin out of her inheritance?'

'How do you know about that?' Caitlyn's teeth were chattering now.

'I make it my business to know. Come on, Caitlyn.' He pressed a glass into her hand. 'At least you won't need to use plan B.'

'Plan B?'

'Your *cousin*—' he spat the word out '—the one you omitted to mention, the one who just happened to be dating my brother when he died, just paid me a little visit…'

'Please, you don't know what she's like…' Caitlyn begged. 'You don't know what she's capable of…'

'Oh, but I do!' he roared. 'How many chances have I given you? How many times have I tried to ignore your lies?' His voice was ominously calm now. 'So innocent…' He chinked his glass against hers. 'My innocent little virgin, who just happened to be on the pill.'

'They're for my spots…'

She shuddered. She didn't have to justify herself to him—didn't have to tell him anything. Her shaking hand placed her glass on the table, spilling champagne. She was trying to leave, only her legs wouldn't move.

'You lie to the bank, lie on your résumé. It comes so naturally I'm sure you don't even know when you're doing it. Hey, Caitlyn—when you told Roxanne you'd get me, did you really believe it? When you cut out my photo from a magazine…?'

Her cheeks were burning, humiliation seeping into her

bone marrow. It was like being stuck in a nightmare, her mouth opening to speak but the words not coming out.

'When you set your little cap at the big prize, did you honestly think you'd win? Did you honestly think I wouldn't see through you? Did you really think that by announcing things to the press you could push me into marrying you? Didn't you realise that I'd only ever marry a woman I love—and that was never, could never, be you.'

'I'm going.' Her voice was a mere croak, her legs like jelly, but at least they were moving.

'Good!' Lazzaro snarled, and he was already ahead of her, brushing past her as he stormed out. 'Get your things and then get the hell out. You've got five minutes—I don't want a single thing of yours left behind. You make me sick.'

'I hate you!' she screamed out at him. Her voice was back now, and there was agony, truth, in every word. 'And I wish to God I'd never fallen in love with you!'

She watched his shoulders stiffen, could see his knuckles white on the handle of the door for just a second—and then he slammed it closed behind him.

There would be time for tears later—but right now, after her outburst, she was numb, frozen, mute. She shook as she stood in the office, trembling at the task in hand, then moved, heart pounding, on a strange kind of autopilot—picking up her things, her books, her pens, her overnight bag that was permanently packed in case they jetted off at a second's notice… There were things to leave too. She pulled out her purse, put down the credit card, wondered what to do with the phone. But it was too much to think about, too hard to stand and delete messages. Somebody else would have to deal with those.

'You've served your purpose, then?' Malvolio stood in the doorway, and she was too numb to be shocked at the sight of him. 'The great Ranaldi's tossing you out?'

'Your brother-in-law's a bastard!' Caitlyn retorted. Her mind was just not there. Her brain was hypothermic, frozen by Lazzaro's brutal words, all her responses slower, her thought processes functioning at basic survival level.

'I could have told you that and saved you the trouble.' Malvolio came over, smiled down at her sympathetically. 'The Ranaldis are all bastards—or bitches,' he added. 'We're not good enough for any of them…'

Her defences were utterly down. She wasn't seeing the red flags that were waving, wasn't hearing the frantic urgent alert as her brain struggled to hit her warning bell. And then she did. Like a fog horn screaming in the darkness, suddenly she heard it, and panic, fear, was gripping her. Only it was just a little bit too late. She could taste the whisky on the mouth that crushed hers, the putridness of his breath, the blood on her lips. There was hate and anger in him as he wedged his body against her—and she knew, *knew* what was going to happen. Knew that even though she was kicking and screaming, his hate was stronger. And as he slammed her to the ground all she could hope was that it would be quick.

That this hell would soon be over.

CHAPTER TWELVE

WHAT the hell had he done?

Lazzaro paced the lobby, his hand clamped over his mouth, his breath hyperventilating into his hand, as his staff watched on bemused. Glynn the only one with the nerve to approach him.

'Is everything okay, sir?'

He didn't answer—didn't even hear him. His mind was with Caitlyn, hating what he'd done to her. He could see her in his mind's eye, standing frozen as he'd shamed her, humiliated her—and for what?

Because once she'd wanted him?

Because all this time she'd loved him?

It was like an axe splitting his skull open—and he hated himself more as he remembered *that* night they'd first met. Hell, if he'd had a photo of *her,* if *she'd* been in a magazine...

Roxanne was poison—she twisted things, blurred the truth—and she wasn't Caitlyn.

Just as he wasn't Luca, so Roxanne wasn't Caitlyn.

Sweet, trusting Caitlyn—which she was.

She *was!*

He trusted her. For the first time in the longest time he

trusted someone—actually believed in someone—and it truly terrified him.

'Sir?' Glynn's face blurred out of focus. 'Is there anything I can get you?' He could see the worry on his manager's face. 'Malvolio was just looking for you—I said you were in your office. Maybe I could call him for you…?'

'Malvolio!'

He was running now, pounding the button for the lift with his hand. Caitlyn *had* been telling the truth. All along she had been telling the truth—and that meant right now *he'd* left her alone with him.

Never had a lift taken so long. Every second as it sped him upwards felt like an hour. Vainly he parted the sliding doors with his hands in frustration in his haste to get to her, racing through the gap and into the hell he'd created—just in time to see her pushed to the floor.

Ripping him off her, slamming him across the room, he knew someone was looking after him—someone up there was looking after him. Because with every fibre of his being he wanted to slam into Malvolio, to hit him, to rip him a new face. But if he did, he knew he'd kill him.

He'd kill him.

His fingers were somehow pressing the security alert button, and that tiny pause was long enough to regroup, to see her sitting on the floor, hugging her knees, to acknowledge that he'd got there in time. And then he faced the bastard—only Lazzaro wasn't the only one filled with hate. Malvolio had his share too.

Screaming like a demented woman, his eyes bulged in fury. 'You think you're so good. Your whole family thinks it's better—you're users—'

'Shut it.' Lazzaro was in his face, but Malvolio wasn't to be contained.

'You swan around like God on the day of reckoning—judging us, shaming us, humiliating us. No wonder Luca hated you!'

Security was there then, already alerted by Glynn. And Lazzaro's office was a ball of chaos for a while—but only a little while. Lazzaro cleared them all out quickly, for which Caitlyn was grateful—because she didn't want to see Malvolio ever again. She would make statements and all that later. Just not right now.

Sitting on the edge of the plump sofa, holding a tissue to her lip, Caitlyn watched as he closed the door, stared at him as he came over to comfort her—stopped him with her eyes as she delivered her words.

'He's right.'

'Caitlyn—'

'Everything Malvolio said is right.'

'Don't—'

'All I ever did wrong was fall in love with you, and you took something nice, something pure, then turned around and shamed me with it.'

'Don't talk about that now.' His usually strong voice was a croak. 'I need to know that you're okay. Did he hurt you anywhere else, apart from your lip?'

'*He* didn't hurt me!' Caitlyn shouted. 'At least nowhere near as much as you did. You made me feel cheaper and dirtier and more ashamed than Malvolio just did...'

'I'm sorry...' He tried to take her hand but she pulled it away. 'I was coming back to say I was sorry.'

'Well, you were already too late.' On surprisingly steady

legs she stood up. 'I've forgiven you so many times, Lazzaro—and I swear I never will again. I swear that I'll hate you for ever.'

Friends were golden.

Real friends. Because, even if he'd started as a colleague, Glynn *was* actually a friend. He came without question when she buzzed him, put his arm around her and led her out as Lazzaro stood there. He drove her home and poured her some wine and called in the troops—an army of friends who swarmed like butterflies, who held her hand every step of the horrible way and told her over and over, till she almost believed it, that none of this was her fault—that she was absolutely better off without him.

CHAPTER THIRTEEN

Ask your cousin.

During the grim post-mortem that came at the end of any romance—where you bargained with yourself and beat yourself up over the *mistakes* that actually weren't mistakes, were just you—in the sleepless nights when you rang your voicemail just to hear his voice, replaying every conversation in a futile search for the clue that's going to unlock the mystery of what went wrong, Caitlyn actually found one. She heard for the first time not just the agony but the loathing in his voice as he'd said it—felt again his hand pushing hers away as she touched his pain and he shut her out.

'Ask your cousin.'

So she did.

She reacquainted herself with her wardrobe and her make-up bag, and stepped out like a foal on wobbly legs, into a world that seemed just a little too bright and loud, and bravely asked the question she had to.

She'd sworn she'd never go back to him.

Would never set foot in the hotel again, would never be

in the same room with Lazzaro Ranaldi as long as there was a breath left in her.

She'd sat and drunk and cried with friends, had read the self-help books and grudgingly accepted that he just 'wasn't that into her'—she had done all the things a girl had to do when she'd had her heart ripped out and stomped on: rung friends instead of him, deleted his mobile number so she wasn't tempted to text him in the middle of the night, removed him from her inbox. And she'd waited.

Waited to feel better.

To believe that time healed.

That one guy didn't fit all.

That of course there were others.

Millions and millions of others, walking the globe at this very minute...

But there was only one *him*.

Only one man who could literally stop her heart as she walked into the hotel bar and saw him sitting there. Only one man she'd actually have done this for—whether it made her brave or stupid that when he'd called her and asked that they might meet she'd agreed.

For closure.

Closure for him as much as for her.

'Thank you.' It was impossible to look him in the eye when he greeted her—impossible, because if she did she'd start crying. 'Thank you for coming.'

'It's fine.' She'd insisted they meet in the bar, unable to face his office. 'I'm sorry it's so public. I just couldn't face the...'

She couldn't even say it—couldn't stand to go back to the office where it had all happened.

Lazzaro understood. 'I know how you feel.'

'I know you do.' She gave a tight smile, because he must—because she didn't actually know how *he* did it, how he sat in the same office not just where Malvolio had been so vile, but where he'd fought so bitterly with Luca.

Why he put himself through it.

Even if Caitlyn couldn't look him in the eye, still she could see the pain etched on his face. The scar that was gouged on his cheek was red and livid today—as if the hell, the cesspit of demons inside, were all clamouring surface-wards now. She wasn't conceited enough to consider it had anything to do with her—she knew his rivers of pain went far deeper than that.

'How's Antonia?' That wasn't why she was here, they both knew that, but she wanted to know. She cared for the other woman whose life had been upended.

'She's doing very well.' Lazzaro managed a small smile at Caitlyn's surprised expression at his upbeat response. 'She really is. The marriage wasn't good—well, we knew that. But it turned out she knew it too. Not about the affairs, of course...'

'Affairs?'

Lazzaro nodded. 'It would seem that when you stumble on the truth you find a lot of untruths.'

'Who said that?' Caitlyn frowned as she tried to recall.

'I did.' Lazzaro gave a tight smile. 'Very Zen of me.'

God, why did he—*how* could he—still make her laugh? How, on this, the blackest of days, in the midst of an impossible conversation, when nothing about this was easy or right, could he, even if for just a second, manage to eke out a laugh?

'She really is okay,' Lazzaro continued. 'It turns out that

she had wanted to end it for a long time—only she didn't know how, didn't feel she had enough reason to walk out on her marriage.'

'Now she has.'

'She is sorry for what happened, and concerned for you too.'

'She doesn't blame me?' Tears that had been held firmly in check couldn't be contained now. A big fat one was rolling down her cheek, and she quickly wiped it away—but it was a pointless exercise, because when he answered her, when this usually distant, emotionally absent man spoke, the softness, the tenderness in his voice, was so unexpected, so laced with the right words, it lacerated her.

Not just what he said, but the fact that it was him saying it.

'You have nothing to feel guilty for. You did nothing wrong, Caitlyn. Antonia knows that, and so must you.'

'I do know that.' She nodded, because now—hearing him say it, knowing Antonia had said it—finally she did.

'I should have taken your first complaint more seriously…'

'No!' She shook her head, because that really was pointless. 'It's done now. I'm just glad that Antonia's okay.'

'She is. She said…' His voice trailed off and Caitlyn frowned.

'Said what?'

'It doesn't matter.' Oh, but it did to Caitlyn. But he shook his head, that part of the conversation clearly over. Which brought them to the next, and Lazzaro swallowed hard before he spoke again. 'I owe you an explanation.'

'You do?'

A muscle was pounding in his cheek, his face was moist with perspiration and his tongue moved to moisten dry lips. When that didn't work, Caitlyn watched as he drained his drink in one gulp. She could almost feel his fight or flight response, knew that he might just stand up and walk out. Because she was feeling it too—was sitting there with her neck so rigid, her nerves so taut, that at any moment she could walk out too—just not go ahead with this appalling conversation.

Only Lazzaro didn't get up and walk out. He sat there and faced it, and so too must Caitlyn.

'After I offered you the job I found out you were Roxanne's cousin. From that moment on…'

'You were waiting for me to reveal my true colours?'

Bitter with regret, he nodded. 'I didn't want to like you, knew that I must never trust you…only more and more I did. When Roxanne came that day, told me about your legal battle when you hadn't even mentioned it…'

'What would you have done, Lazzaro?'

'I would have helped.'

'No.' Caitlyn shook her head. 'That would have proved to you that I was using you. My mother grew up in that house. Apart from a couple of years when she had me, she's lived there all her life. She's renovated it, decorated it, furnished it…'

'You don't have to explain…'

'You've made it so that I do,' Caitlyn pointed out. 'It wasn't about money—and it wasn't even about the house. It was about her home. My mum offered to Cheryl to leave it in her will equally to both Roxanne and I…'

'I misjudged you.'

'You did.'

'I have misjudged many things—you see, Roxanne and
I…'

His hand tightened on the glass he was holding, and she
wanted, *how* she wanted, to reach out and hold it, to
comfort him, console him somehow as he served up his
wretched past. Only it wasn't her place any more.

Never had been her place, Caitlyn realised, because
Lazzaro had seen to that.

Lazzaro had refused to let anyone in.

'There was an incident,' Lazzaro bravely started. 'One
that didn't reach the newspapers. When he came to my
office, I told Luca that I had arranged rehab for him, that
I would stand by him so long as he made some attempt to
sort himself out—only he wouldn't go.' His voice was surprisingly calm—resigned, even. 'He just wouldn't accept
there was a problem—but everyone could see it. His
drinking, the gambling—he had debts everywhere. I was
running around cleaning up the messes he was leaving
behind him, and I just couldn't do it for ever…'

'Of course you couldn't.' Caitlyn's voice was strong.
'He had to acknowledge it before he could get help…' But
that wasn't the issue today, and they both knew it.

'Roxanne turned up as he was leaving. He sort of pushed
past her and knocked her over. She was upset—we were both
upset. I helped her up and she started crying, so I comforted
her…' It was as if he were giving a police statement, his
voice unnervingly even as he reeled off the appalling train
of events, delivered brutal words in an impassive tone. 'I told
her I was sorry for all Luca was putting her through…'

It was Caitlyn whose throat was dry now, and she was

grateful when he picked up her bottle of water and topped up her glass. She took a sip, but just about missed her mouth because her hands were trembling so much.

'I started kissing her, telling her I would treat her so much better than Luca... Things were getting a bit out of hand, and then...'

'Luca came back?' Caitlyn finished for him.

'Luca caught us.'

'That's when he hit you?'

'He went crazy...said that I had always been the better one, the older one, the smarter one, that I had screwed up his life, that I had taken everything good from him and now I was taking the woman he loved, that I'd humiliated him over and over...' He pinched the bridge of his nose, screwed his eyes closed as he relieved that hell. 'He said quite a lot more than just that.'

'I'm sure he did.'

'Then he stormed off. And I went to the hospital to get stitched.'

Caitlyn watched, tears streaming down her face, as he gagged out an expletive and this strongest of men almost fell apart.

And for the first time he faced it.

As if a fist had gone into his stomach, he let out a shudder of breath, almost doubled up in agony—and he told her. Or did he? Because he truly didn't know if he was talking it or living it again. At that point he wasn't sitting with Caitlyn, he was back pacing in that hospital cubicle, a wad of gauze pressed to his cheek, so incredibly angry he was climbing the walls. He just wanted the hell out of there, wanted to get stitched so he could go and find Luca, to make things right, to fix his brother. Then everything had just faded into oblivion. Aghast, he'd watched as a stretcher whizzed past his cubicle. It was as if he was looking at himself in a mirror, and he'd seen the horror on his own face mistaken by a nurse, who'd pulled his curtain tightly closed. Only Lazzaro had opened it, striding into the re-suscitation area despite the protests of the staff. Their angry shouts had been dim in his ears, theirs the shocked expressions as they'd looked down at the body they were working on and seen it was the mirror image of this intruder who had marched in. And he had seen the wretchedness in the doctors' eyes as they'd realised he was his twin.

'I'm so sorry.'

Paltry words that had been delivered by a doctor even before Antonia had arrived.

He hadn't even needed a local anaesthetic when they'd sutured him—his whole body had been numb with pain as he'd lain on the hospital trolley and the needle had slid in and out of his flesh.

'I'm so sorry.'

Paltry words that had been delivered hours later, as he'd held his brother's cold blue hand, had stared at a face that might as well have been his—had felt as if it *was* his.

'I knew he was dead the moment I saw him…' The tirade that had spewed from his mouth abated a touch, and still Caitlyn listened. 'I knew he was dead, and that nothing they were going to do would bring him back. It was over by the time Antonia arrived, and then my mother…'

'Roxanne too?' Caitlyn checked, and he nodded.

'Antonia called her. She didn't know at that point what had happened.'

'But you told her?'

'Roxanne did.' Lazzaro let out a long breath. 'She was hysterical. She said that we'd as good as killed him, that if I hadn't come on to her, that if he hadn't caught us…' His skin was grey, the lines around his eyes so dark they looked as if they might have been pencilled in. 'He came back, Caitlyn. God, he came back—and maybe he was going to get help. Maybe if we hadn't been—'

'Maybe he'd forgotten his car keys,' Caitlyn snapped back, surprising even herself with her bitterness. But she was cross—cross with Luca, the Saint Luca Ranaldi he had somehow become, the man who in death had been excused his mistakes, exempted by his brother, by his family, for his appalling leading role in all of this—who'd had so much and been so careless, not just with himself, but with the happiness of those who'd loved him. 'Maybe he'd come back to borrow some more money, or to tell you where to get off.'

'Get off?' Lazzaro frowned. Even if his English was excellent, sometimes he missed a point—but not this time, because Caitlyn wouldn't let him.

'I could put it far less politely—but I think you know what I mean. So, what did your family say?'

'A lot. My mother was hysterical—she hit me…' His voice was void of emotion now—detached, even. 'She actually tore some of the stitches I had just had… Antonia vomited, told me she would hate me for ever, would hate Roxanne too—I told them it wasn't her fault…' He gave a mirthless laugh. 'There are a lot of people who will hate me for ever…hell isn't going to be lonely.'

'I don't hate you, Lazzaro.' She looked at him for just an atom of time, saw the dart in his eyes, the tiny flicker of relief on his tired face. 'Maybe I did at the time, or maybe I just said it to hurt you, but I don't actually hate you now.'

'Thank you.'

Which led to another tear—but only one. What she had to say, what she had to hear, was just too important to lose to emotion. 'That's why you and Roxanne didn't carry on seeing each other afterwards?' Caitlyn continued, watching him, watching every flicker of his reaction. 'Just too much guilt?'

'Of course.'

'Of course,' Caitlyn repeated in a clipped voice, watching again as he frowned at her response. 'I don't believe you, Lazzaro.'

'What are you talking about?'

And for the first time since she'd sat down she *did* manage to look him in the eye and hold it—was able to stare into those dark liquid pools. Because, unlike Lazzaro, she had nothing more to hide now—nothing she couldn't or wouldn't reveal. Hell, she'd already told him she loved him, and had accepted his rejection. Funny, though, that through it all, dignity prevailed—that she, Caitlyn Bell, was actually incredibly strong.

'You're lying.'

'Lying!' His mouth opened incredulously. 'I've been more honest with you than I've ever been. I've told you, *told* you what happened, and you have the gall to sit there and tell me—'

'That you're lying!' Caitlyn finished for him, shouting the words almost, not caring who was watching, who was listening.

'I spoke to Roxanne.' She hurled the words at him. 'I went to the woman I hate more than anyone in the world and I asked *her* what happened *that* day.'

'What did she tell you?'

'The same as you.'

She watched his frown, saw the confusion in his tired eyes.

'Roxanne's a liar—we both know that,' Caitlyn spat, furious not with him, but *for* him. No, she conceded, her mind racing at a million miles an hour, furious *with* him too—for the agony, for the self-infliction of such pain, such guilt. 'And you're a bloody liar, Lazzaro, and you're still making excuses for Luca, still cleaning up the mess he made.'

She stood up, hardly able to believe what she was doing—that she was walking out, walking out when perhaps he needed her the most, that she was furious when perhaps he needed calm. But she couldn't help it—couldn't contain what she was feeling within the parameters that might better fit.

'After everything that's happened, after all I've been through—*with* you, *for* you—you can sit there and look me in the eye and bloody well lie to me. If, after all that, you can still hold back the most essential piece of yourself, then—you know what? I don't actually want the rest.'

'Caitlyn!'

His voice barked at her to come back, ordered her to turn around and not walk out. But she *did* walk out, and she did what you're not supposed to—Caitlyn looked back, just once, and she was actually glad that she had. She saw him sitting there, set in stone, frozen, immutable, and by choice completely alone, by choice refusing to get angry, refusing to see his brother for what he was, refusing to grab at life and move on. It was all the impetus she needed to walk faster—to shake her head in contempt and get the hell out of there. She was walking so fast she was almost running.

She could hear the frantic clipping of her shoes on the polished marble as she dashed through the foyer crying, not in pain but in anger, and she heard him run behind her, tempted, so tempted, to slap him as he grabbed her wrist and spun her around.

'How?' His eyes were livid, his question a howl. 'How do you know?'

'Because I know *you*.' She jabbed the fingers on her free hand into his chest. 'I know you're a callous bastard, and I know that you've got a few scruples missing, but I know, *I know*, that you'd never, ever have stooped that low.'

'How?' He said it again, not livid now, more bewildered. 'How could you know that?'

'You already know that I love you...' Tears were coursing down her face. 'What you've consistently failed to see, though, is that I'm actually a nice person—and I happen to have very good taste...' She even managed a smile as she said it—could smile because *he* actually smiled a bit. 'And I have my standards, and I trust myself, and I just don't think I'd have fallen so hard for someone I couldn't trust. Someone who wouldn't do it to a friend leads me to believe that he would never, *ever* have done it to his own brother.'

'Not here...' His voice was urgent as he glanced around at the lobby—the lobby where they'd started this journey and should probably end it.

Only she couldn't. She conceded one final demand and nodded as he gestured to the lift, joined him as they headed towards the office—and it actually didn't bother her as much as she'd thought it would. Lazzaro's issues were somehow overriding hers.

'Roxanne did come on to me—and I was pushing her off.' He spoke even as the lift took them skywards. They were standing at either side, staring at the door rather than looking at each other. 'I told her to get off—and I am using your polite expression here.' She did look over to him then, and even if it wasn't a big one, there was a small smile as somehow they slipped into their own world, their own language, the bit that was just about them. 'She was all over me—saying she'd always wanted me—she dated Malvolio too, you know…'

The lift door sliding open went unnoticed. Caitlyn was stunned at this revelation, yet as they walked into his office she knew it somehow made sense.

'That was how she met Luca?' Caitlyn asked.

'Malvolio was her ticket to Luca.'

'Unlike me.' She gave a tight shrug. 'I just went straight to the top.'

'Never,' Lazzaro said seriously. 'Never again will I compare you to her.'

'She was even a horrible little girl…' Caitlyn rolled her eyes and let out an angry breath. 'Always messing up my things, breaking my toys—anything I had she wanted. You know, I'm not excusing Malvolio…' Caitlyn was thinking more than talking, thinking out loud. 'But you can see now why he'd hate you so—hate me too…'

'I don't want to think of him at all,' Lazzaro interrupted. 'I don't even want to try and understand his twisted mind.'

And she didn't want to think about him either. She wanted to think about Lazzaro, wanted to try and finally understand.

'Why didn't you tell your family what really happened?'

'So I could humiliate Luca all over again?' Lazzaro shook his head. 'How, with his body still warm, could I tell my family that he had nothing? That the one good thing he thought he had in his life—?'

'So you took the blame for him?' Caitlyn said. 'You let them think that it was you coming on to Roxanne instead of the other way around?'

'Luca said that I took everything from him—maybe I did. I just couldn't take that last piece.'

'Luca blamed you because that's what he did best—blamed you for his mess because it was easier than blaming himself, easier than admitting he had a problem, easier than facing up that his *life* was a mess. Luca knew what had happened as much as *I* know what happened,' Caitlyn responded firmly, nodding her head as he shook his. 'Hell, yes, he was jealous, and he probably wanted to think it was you, but he knew—he knew exactly what happened that day. He just didn't want to face it—the same way he didn't want to face anything…'

'You really think he knew?'

'Absolutely.' And she watched as her words sank in, watched him blink as he opened his eyes to the truth, and it was like watching the clock go back, as if a great, filthy weight was being lifted.

'Oh, Caitlyn…'

He was holding her, holding her so tight, kissing her face, kissing her tears, his hands everywhere—and even if he didn't love her, would never love her, even if she should just push him off, she couldn't. She would rather end it like this than the way it had ended before—would give him this because she needed it too, needed to feel him one more time.

Urgent, frantic sex *was* a great balm. His hands were pushing up her skirt even as hers grappled with his buckle. His mouth was hot on her neck, biting, bruising, thrilling. Lowering her to the floor, he was pushing her, but somehow supporting her, tearing at her stockings, her panties, and Caitlyn's want was as prevalent as his. Pushing down his trousers, feeling his taut buttocks, she was holding him, holding the bit of him that she needed, wanted, adored—and it was beautiful—and it belonged inside her.

With each delicious thrust he called out her name, and somehow he was kissing her too, kissing her, licking her. His shoulders were over her and she was watching him, watching him and trying to capture him, to remember this for ever—and he *had* held back before, because even if the sex had been wonderful, this was *it*—this wasn't him and her, it was *them*, one person almost. And maybe she *had* held back too, Caitlyn realised. He was so deep inside her, his hips grinding into hers, his body filled with a delicious tension that begged release. Perhaps she had held back, but there was no need to now. He knew she loved him; there were no secrets any more.

'Oh, God, Caitlyn.'

He was calling out her name, and she was calling his, until she couldn't, her throat closing on his name before she screamed it out, every muscle in her body tensing, her legs wrapped around him, her thighs dragging him in as he groaned his gift into her, as she accepted it, breathless, dizzy, but amazingly calm.

Afterwards they lay there—holding each other, staring at the ceiling, waiting for the world to come back.

'Every time I look at this room now, instead of thinking about…' He gave a laugh. But it wasn't funny, and it wasn't sad, it was just better.

'You'll remember me, then?'

'Remember you?' He propped himself up on his elbow, stared down at her. And she wasn't crying, she was able to stare right back, to look at him and love him simply because she did. 'I don't have to remember you—I see you every day.'

'You won't be seeing me every day, Lazzaro. It can't work…'

'What was that, then?'

'Sex.' Caitlyn stared bravely back at him. 'Fabulous, wonderful, and much-needed sex.'

'That wasn't *sex;* that was making love.'

'For me it was.' She gave a tight smile. 'But we all know that *you* don't need to love a woman to—'

'I need to love a woman to make love to her like that…' He frowned down at her. 'You were really going to walk away—after that?' He shook his head in wonder. 'You know, you're a strange girl, Caitlyn…' He kissed the tip of her nose. 'A very good girl who is actually a very bad girl too.'

'But in a good way?' Caitlyn sniffed. She wasn't actually thinking about that now. Her mind was trying to concentrate, to focus on what he'd just said, and her heart that had just slowed down was tripping into tachycardia again as she wrestled with the impossible. 'What you said about loving…?'

'I meant it.'

'Meant what?' Caitlyn asked gingerly, nibbling on her bottom lip, scared to check, scared to ask, in case she didn't like the answer, scared to even hope.

'That I love you.'

'Oh.'

'I love you,' he said again.

'Me?'

'Yes, you.'

'Say it again.'

'I love you.'

'So, what does that mean?'

He smiled down at her, massaging her raw and bruised ego with his eyes and words, and she let him. She needed to hear it. 'That I don't want to be without you—ever.'

'And?'

'That I want to wake up to you in the morning. I want you to annoy the hell out of me. I want you to confuse me—I don't ever want to know you—'

'That doesn't make sense,' Caitlyn interrupted. 'What you meant to say was that you *want* to know me…'

'I know exactly what I am saying. I want to spend the rest of my life trying to work you out. I love that you confuse me.'

'Oh.' Caitlyn smiled, closing her eyes—because she could now, because she knew that when she opened them he'd still be there.

'In fact I fell in love with you a long time ago.'

'When?' Her eyes were still closed, and she was smiling, his words like the warm sun on her face. 'At the hotel? Or was it in Rome…?'

'Shut up and let me talk.'

So she did just that. And she was so, so glad that she did, or she might never have heard his amazing answer.

'On the stroke of midnight the night we first met.'

'It wasn't midnight.' She opened her eyes and her heart to him. She couldn't be quiet, just couldn't contain it. Because it was just so wonderful, so amazing, that he'd felt it too—that love, *their* love, had always been real, that the torch she'd carried for him had had heavy-duty batteries for a very good reason. 'It was ten to twelve. Because I specifically remember looking at the clock. It was at ten minutes to twelve that we fell in love.'

'Just because you move fast, it doesn't mean that I have to… I like to take my time and think about these things.' He kissed her, kissed her between sentences—like a gorgeous long meal, like a wonderful smorgasbord, where you didn't have to rush, could just pick and choose the good bits and go back for more whenever you wanted. You could start and finish with dessert if you wanted, or just get full on a thousand prawns. 'I went into the ballroom and everyone was talking. I had friends around me, a good malt whisky in my hand and a beautiful woman on my arm, and I looked at my watch, and I looked at the closed door, and I wanted to be on the other side of it. I had everything a man could want—only it didn't feel right because you weren't there.'

'I'm here now,' Caitlyn said softly.

'So am I…' He rained her face with butterfly kisses, and she rained them back, kissing away all the hurt and the grief, chasing away all the horrible, scary shadows till there was only light left. 'I'm here, where I belong.'

EPILOGUE

'DO YOU want me to say something?' Caitlyn offered as Lazzaro called for the bill.

'The food was fantastic,' Lazzaro said. 'Let's not make a fuss.'

'But every time we come here they get it wrong! I specifically ordered the mushroom risotto, and we got vegetarian arranchini.'

Lazzaro peeled off another note and added it to his already generous tip. They were sitting in one of the smartest cafés in Rome, and the waiter had in fact done an amazing job—deciphering somehow, from Caitlyn's truly appalling Italian, that they wanted rice and vegetables.

It *was* bad.

Even after a year of flying between two amazing cities—even after having a son who had been born here in Rome—Caitlyn's mastery of the language was poor, to say the least. But her Italian was delivered with such flair, such passion and enthusiasm, and such a warm, generous smile, that no one—not the doctors, nor the midwives, nor the hotel staff or even a waiter—had the heart to tell her.

'*Che era meraviglioso—grazie.*' Caitlyn beamed at the

bemused waiter as she clipped little Dante into his pram and wheeled him out of the restaurant.

'That was wonderful—thank you…' Lazzaro loosely translated, rolling his eyes and mouthing another thank-you to the waiter, then joining his wife and new son on the street outside.

'You'd think they'd never seen a blond baby.' Caitlyn smiled as everyone who passed cooed into the stroller. 'Mind you—he *is* gorgeous.'

And the image of Caitlyn.

Blond, already lifting his head and taking in the world, smiling and cooing at six weeks and refusing to sleep, he was a carbon copy of his mother—and Lazzaro, just as he was with his wife, was completely smitten.

'Right—time to look for a gift. I still don't get why some people don't have a bridal registry,' Lazzaro said as they wandered the streets.

'We didn't…' Caitlyn pointed out.

'Because you refused to—and just look at the pile of rubbish we ended up with.' Lazzaro stared moodily into a gallery. 'She's been married already—she got everything she wanted the first time around…'

'And she got everything she wanted in the divorce.' Caitlyn giggled. 'How about that?' she asked, pointing to a painting in the window of the modern art gallery.

'It could have been done by a five-year-old—in fact, give Dante a brush and he could do better.'

'It's divine,' Caitlyn breathed.

'It's three circles within a circle.'

'Antonia, Marianna and baby Luca, and circling them, looking out for them, is Dario.'

'I still think the wedding should be at Ranaldi's.' Lazzaro was still staring at the picture and trying to see what she saw—trying to work out Caitlyn's impossible, crazy take on the world, trying to take in that Antonia was marrying his friend Alberto's son. 'I would have done it better.'

'Probably.' Caitlyn shrugged. 'But I'd never have seen you—you'd have spent the night marching around the kitchen insisting everything was "the best". This way, you get to enjoy yourself…' She was suddenly serious. 'Anyway, Alberto is enjoying organising it—it's good to see him happy after the year he's had.'

'I know,' Lazzaro conceded.

'And talking of weddings…' A mischievous smile was on her lips, but two circles of red were burning on her cheeks as she broached a terribly taboo subject. 'Can you believe Roxanne and Malvolio sent us an invitation to theirs? Can you believe they actually invited us?'

They were inside the gallery now. Lazzaro was ignoring the owner's effusive attempts to discuss the delightful piece they were buying—instead handing over his credit card and giving the details as to where it should be sent.

'They deserve each other!' Lazzaro hissed as they stepped outside.

'Well, they've got each other.' Caitlyn laughed. 'Thanks in small part to me. Did I tell you I hexed her?'

'Hexed her?' Lazzaro frowned—he was pushing the stroller now, guiding it down the bumpy steps as Caitlyn clipped alongside, and this time he wasn't pretending not to understand—he honestly didn't. ·

'I wrapped her name around a piece of garlic and stuck it in the freezer—she's getting her just deserts!'

'You're telling me that you put a spell on her?'

'Just a little one.' Caitlyn pouted. 'Wishes do come true, you know.'

'Then make one.'

They were back at the Trevi Fountain and Lazzaro was rummaging in his pocket for loose change. Only Caitlyn didn't need to waste a wish—didn't need to wish on a coin or a star, or cut up pictures—because she knew without wishing that they'd be back for more, knew without question that they were in this for ever.

'Go on,' Lazzaro prompted, holding out a coin, but Caitlyn shook her head.

'I've got all my wishes—how about you?'

'Just one…' He tossed the coin into the fountain, then pulled her towards him as only Lazzaro could. 'A girl.'

'A girl?'

'Or a boy.' Lazzaro shrugged. 'I want another mini-you.'

'It might be a mini-*you* this time.'

'I don't care.' Lazzaro laughed, as he did often these days. 'Let's just go and make another baby.'

* * * * *

Turn the page for a sneak preview of
AFTERSHOCK, *a new anthology*
featuring New York Times *bestselling author*
Sharon Sala.

Available October 2008.

n⬤cturne™

Dramatic and sensual tales of paranormal romance.

Chapter 1

October
New York City

Nicole Masters was sitting cross-legged on her sofa while a cold autumn rain peppered the windows of her fourth-floor apartment. She was poking at the ice cream in her bowl and trying not to be in a mood.

Six weeks ago, a simple trip to her neighborhood pharmacy had turned into a nightmare. She'd walked into the middle of a robbery. She never even saw the man who shot her in the head and left her for dead. She'd survived, but some of her senses had not. She was dealing with short-term memory loss and a tendency to stagger. Even though she'd been told the problems were most likely temporary, she waged a daily battle with depression.

Her parents had been killed in a car wreck when she was twenty-one. And except for a few friends—and most recently her boyfriend, Dominic Tucci, who lived in the apartment right above hers, she was alone. Her doctor kept reminding her that she should be grateful to be alive, and on one level she knew he was right. But he wasn't living in her shoes.

If she'd been anywhere else but at that pharmacy when the robbery happened, she wouldn't have died twice on the way to the hospital. Instead of being grateful that she'd survived, she couldn't stop thinking of what she'd lost.

But that wasn't the end of her troubles. On top of everything else, something strange was happening inside her head. She'd begun to hear odd things: sounds, not voices— at least, she didn't think it was voices. It was more like the distant noise of rapids—a rush of wind and water inside her head that, when it came, blocked out everything around her. It didn't happen often, but when it did, it was frightening, and it was driving her crazy.

The blank moments, which is what she called them, even had a rhythm. First there came that sound, then a cold sweat, then panic with no reason. Part of her feared it was the beginning of an emotional breakdown. And part of her feared it wasn't—that it was going to turn out to be a permanent souvenir of her resurrection.

Frustrated with herself and the situation as it stood, she upped the sound on the TV remote. But instead of *Wheel of Fortune,* an announcer broke in with a special bulletin.

"This just in. Police are on the scene of a kidnapping that occurred only hours ago at The Dakota. Molly Dane, the six-year-old daughter of one of Hollywood's blockbuster stars, Lyla Dane, was taken by force from the family apartment. At this time they have yet to receive a ransom demand. The housekeeper was seriously injured during the abduction, and is, at the present time, in surgery. Police are hoping to be able to talk to her once she regains consciousness. In the meantime, we are going now to a press conference with Lyla Dane."

Horrified, Nicole stilled as the cameras went live to where the actress was speaking before a bank of microphones. The shock and terror in Lyla Dane's voice were physically painful to watch. But even though Nicole kept upping the volume, the sound continued to fade.

Just when she was beginning to think something was wrong with her set, the broadcast suddenly switched from the Dane press conference to what appeared to be footage of the kidnapping, beginning with footage from inside the apartment.

When the front door suddenly flew back against the wall and four men rushed in, Nicole gasped. Horrified, she quickly realized that this must have been caught on a security camera inside the Dane apartment.

As Nicole continued to watch, a small Asian woman, who she guessed was the maid, rushed forward in an effort to keep them out. When one of the men hit her in the face with his gun, Nicole moaned. The violence was too reminiscent of what she'd lived through. Sick to her stomach, she fisted her hands against her belly, wishing it was over, but unable to tear her gaze away.

When the maid dropped to the carpet, the same man followed with a vicious kick to the little woman's midsection that lifted her off the floor.

"Oh, my God," Nicole said. When blood began to pool beneath the maid's head, she started to cry.

As the tape played on, the four men split up in different directions. The camera caught one running down a

long marble hallway, then disappearing into a room.
Moments later he reappeared, carrying a little girl, who
Nicole assumed was Molly Dane. The child was wearing
a pair of red pants and a white turtleneck sweater, and her
hair was partially blocking her abductor's face as he carried
her down the hall. She was kicking and screaming in his
arms, and when he slapped her, it elicited an agonized
scream that brought the other three running. Nicole
watched in horror as one of them ran up and put his hand
over Molly's face. Seconds later, she went limp.

One moment they were in the foyer, then they were gone.

Nicole jumped to her feet, then staggered drunkenly.
The bowl of ice cream she'd absentmindedly placed in her
lap shattered at her feet, splattering glass and melting ice
cream everywhere.

The picture on the screen abruptly switched from the kidnapping to what Nicole assumed was a rerun of Lyla Dane's
plea for her daughter's safe return, but she was numb.

Before she could think what to do next, the doorbell
rang. Startled by the unexpected sound, she shakily swiped
at the tears and took a step forward. She didn't feel the glass
shards piercing her feet until she took the second step. At
that point, sharp pains shot through her foot. She gasped,
then looked down in confusion. Her legs looked as if she'd
been running through mud, and she was standing in broken
glass and ice cream, while a thin ribbon of blood seeped
out from beneath her toes.

"Oh, no," Nicole mumbled, then stifled a second moan
of pain.

The doorbell rang again. She shivered, then clutched her
head in confusion.

"Just a minute!" she yelled, then tried to sidestep the rest of the debris as she hobbled to the door.

When she looked through the peephole in the door, she didn't know whether to be relieved or regretful.

It was Dominic, and as usual, she was a mess.

Nicole smiled a little self-consciously as she opened the door to let him in. "I just don't know what's happening to me. I think I'm losing my mind."

"Hey, don't talk about my woman like that."

Nicole rode the surge of delight his words brought. "So I'm still your woman?"

Dominic lowered his head.

Their lips met.

The kiss proceeded.

Slowly.

Thoroughly.

* * * * *

Be sure to look for the AFTERSHOCK *anthology next month, as well as other exciting paranormal stories from Silhouette Nocturne.*
Available in October wherever books are sold.

▼ Silhouette®

SPECIAL EDITION™

**FROM *NEW YORK TIMES*
BESTSELLING AUTHOR**

LINDA LAEL MILLER

A STONE CREEK CHRISTMAS

Veterinarian Olivia O'Ballivan finds the animals in Stone Creek playing Cupid between her and Tanner Quinn. Even Tanner's daughter, Sophie, is eager to play matchmaker. With everyone conspiring against them and the holiday season fast approaching, Tanner and Olivia may just get everything they want for Christmas after all!

*Available December 2008
wherever books are sold.*

kept for his *Pleasure*

She's his mistress on demand

Whether seduction takes place in his king-size bed,
a five-star hotel, his office or beachside penthouse,
these fabulously wealthy, charismatic and sexy men
know how to keep a woman coming back for more!
Commitment might not be high on his agenda—or
even on it at all!

She's his mistress on demand—but when he wants her
body and soul, he will be demanding a whole lot more!
Dare we say it...even marriage!

Available in October

HOUSEKEEPER AT HIS BECK AND CALL
by Susan Stephens
#2769

Don't miss any books in this exciting new miniseries
from Presents!

Coming next month:

TAKEN BY THE BAD BOY
by Kelly Hunter #2778

HARLEQUIN *Presents*

THE MEDITERRANEAN PRINCES

Playboy princes, island brides—
bedded and wedded by royal command!

Roman and Nico Magnati—
Mediterranean princes with undisputed
playboy reputations!

These powerfully commanding princes expect their
every command to be instantly obeyed—and they're not
afraid to use their well-practiced seduction to get want
they want, when they want it....

Available in October

HIS MAJESTY'S MISTRESS
by *Robyn Donald*
#2768

Don't miss the second story in Robyn's brilliant duet,
available next month!:

THE MEDITERRANEAN PRINCE'S
CAPTIVE VIRGIN
#2776

REQUEST YOUR FREE BOOKS!

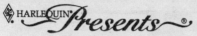 

2 FREE NOVELS PLUS 2 FREE GIFTS!

YES! Please send me 2 FREE Harlequin Presents® novels and my 2 FREE gifts (gifts are worth about $10). After receiving them, if I don't wish to receive any more books, I can return the shipping statement marked "cancel". If I don't cancel, I will receive 6 brand-new novels every month and be billed just $4.05 per book in the U.S. or $4.74 per book in Canada, plus 25¢ shipping and handling per book and applicable taxes, if any*. That's a savings of close to 15% off the cover price! I understand that accepting the 2 free books and gifts places me under no obligation to buy anything. I can always return a shipment and cancel at any time. Even if I never buy another book, the two free books and gifts are mine to keep forever.   106 HDN ERRW 306 HDN ERRL

Name	(PLEASE PRINT)	
Address		Apt. #
City	State/Prov.	Zip/Postal Code

Signature (if under 18, a parent or guardian must sign)

* Terms and prices subject to change without notice. N.Y. residents add applicable sales tax. Canadian residents will be charged applicable provincial taxes and GST. Offer not valid in Quebec. This offer is limited to one order per household. All orders subject to approval. Credit or debit balances in a customer's account(s) may be offset by any other outstanding balance owed by or to the customer. Please allow 4 to 6 weeks for delivery. Offer available while quantities last.

Your Privacy: Harlequin Books is committed to protecting your privacy. Our Privacy Policy is available online at www.eHarlequin.com or upon request from the Reader Service. From time to time we make our lists of customers available to reputable third parties who may have a product or service of interest to you. If you would prefer we not share your name and address, please check here. ☐

HP08R

I ♥

HARLEQUIN *Presents*

BROUGHT TO YOU BY FANS OF
HARLEQUIN PRESENTS.

We are its editors and authors
and biggest fans—and we'd
love to hear from YOU!

Subscribe today to our online blog at
www.iheartpresents.com

MEDITERRANEAN DOCTORS

Demanding, devoted and
drop-dead gorgeous—
These Latin doctors will
make your heart race!

Smolderingly sexy Mediterranean doctors

Saving lives by day…red-hot lovers by night

**Read these four Mediterranean Doctors stories
in this new collection by your favorite authors,
available in Presents EXTRA October 2008:**

THE SICILIAN DOCTOR'S MISTRESS
by SARAH MORGAN

THE ITALIAN COUNT'S BABY
by AMY ANDREWS

SPANISH DOCTOR, PREGNANT NURSE
by CAROL MARINELLI

THE SPANISH DOCTOR'S LOVE-CHILD
by KATE HARDY